Tory reached into her bag and took out the hunting knife her dad had given her.

A sound at the other end of the alley had her turning. She slipped away from Ben, further into the shadows to give him a clear shot at the assailants. They let out a burst of semi-automatic fire and dived for cover.

Ben moved left and she took the right side. She watched him blend seamlessly into the darkness. She closed her eyes and focused her senses, listening for things that were out of place. She heard it then, the rustle of cloth against the building.

She just made out the silhouette of a man with an assault rifle crouched low to the ground, waiting for her or Ben to make a mistake.

As soon as he scanned away from her, Tory moved. Quickly she ran forward and attacked him from the back. Holding her knife to his throat, she growled, "Drop your weapon."

Her grip slipped and the man lifted his gun.

Available in December 2006
from Silhouette Sensation

Exclusive

KATHERINE GARBERA

1373462z

DID YOU PURCHASE THIS BOOK WITHOUT A COVER?
If you did, you should be aware it is **stolen property** as it was
reported *unsold and destroyed* by a retailer. Neither the author nor
the publisher has received any payment for this book.

*All the characters in this book have no existence outside the
imagination of the author, and have no relation whatsoever to anyone
bearing the same name or names. They are not even distantly inspired
by any individual known or unknown to the author, and all the
incidents are pure invention.*

*All Rights Reserved including the right of reproduction in whole or
in part in any form. This edition is published by arrangement with
Harlequin Enterprises II B.V. The text of this publication or any part
thereof may not be reproduced or transmitted in any form or by any
means, electronic or mechanical, including photocopying, recording,
storage in an information retrieval system, or otherwise, without the
written permission of the publisher.*

*This book is sold subject to the condition that it shall not, by way of
trade or otherwise, be lent, resold, hired out or otherwise circulated
without the prior consent of the publisher in any form of binding or
cover other than that in which it is published and without a similar
condition including this condition being imposed on the subsequent
purchaser.*

*Silhouette, Silhouette Sensation and Colophon are registered
trademarks of Harlequin Books S.A., used under licence.*

*First published in Great Britain 2006
Silhouette Books, Eton House, 18-24 Paradise Road,
Richmond, Surrey TW9 1SR*

© Harlequin Books S.A. 2006

*Special thanks and acknowledgement are given to Katherine
Garbera for her contribution to the ATHENA FORCE mini-series.*

*ISBN-13: 978 0 373 51408 3
ISBN-10: 0 373 51408 5*

18-1206

*Printed and bound in Spain
by Litografía Rosés S.A., Barcelona*

KATHERINE GARBERA

is the award-winning, bestselling author of more than twenty-five books. She started making up stories for her own benefit when she was on a competitive swimming team in high school. Katherine holds a red belt in the martial art of Tae Kwon Do and vows that there's not a piece of plywood out there that can take her in a fair match! Readers can visit her on the web at www.katherinegarbera.com.

To my kick-ass gal pals—Beverly Brandt, Eve Gaddy, Nancy Thompson and Mary Louise Wells—who make the adventure of writing such a fun one.

Acknowledgements

A huge thank you to Cindy Dees for answering every question imaginable pertaining to the military and for doing it so quickly. Any mistakes are my own.
Also thanks to all the writers in the Slave Away Café whose shared company made it easier to write this book!

Chapter 1

Ben Forsythe was having a crappy day.

He'd been in meetings virtually all day and now, when he finally had a free moment to dial Tory Patton's number, he got her voice mail. He rubbed the back of his neck and almost hung up without leaving a message. He couldn't tell her where he was, didn't know when he could call again. But he needed to hear her voice. Needed for just a second to remember who was waiting for him at home.

"Babe," he said, just to needle her, "it's me. Don't know when I'll be able to call again. Be good."

He hung up. He had e-mail available but seldom

used it because his team was always on the move and he didn't want to leave an electronic trail of where they'd been.

It was dry and blazing hot in late June in the desert of Berzhaan and he was sick to death of sand. He shaded his eyes and wished for a minute that he was a different man. The kind who could walk away and never look back. The kind who could blithely go about his everyday life and never know that there were men and women who were risking their lives to enable that.

But he wasn't.

Ben's father had been an undercover CIA agent, a man whose government's only acknowledgment of his death overseas while on an assignment was a star and a date on a wall. Ben was starting to think that he wanted more than that at the end of his days.

He entered the makeshift command center and awaited his orders. He worked for a covert military group called LASER, the Lost Airman's Service. Their mandate was simple and focused—they rescued servicemen who were being held prisoner in hostile places. They used whatever means were necessary to bring them home.

With the help of AA.gov, a Web site and organization whose main function was to keep alumni of the Athena Academy for the Advancement of

Women in touch with one another, but whose covert side included certain spy missions, he'd embedded one of his men with a television news crew. The lead reporter, Andrea Jancey, was Tory's protégé at UBC. She and Tory had both attended the prestigious Athena Academy. Andrea had the same skills that Tory did, which meant she could handle herself in almost any situation. Ben had a lot of respect for the Athena grads he knew, including his own sister, Alex.

For this mission, Ben was using Andrea and her news crew to get close to the insurgents fighting in the desert of Berzhaan. His intel had identified a group under Kemeni rebel leader Al Ahib as having captured two Marine pilots. The Kemeni were down in strength at the moment, but highly uncooperative with the U.S. Ben's team was in country to get the pilots out. He had a small team of seven men. They'd worked together for a long time and knew each other well.

"Any word from Manning?" he asked Lewis Salvo, their communications guru. Salvo managed the satellite, navigation/GPS and emergency radios. Ben had seen him coax a waterlogged radio back into action. If anyone could raise a signal on Manning, it was Salvo.

Salvo didn't glance up from the frequencies he

was monitoring on their personal radios. "Nothing yet, he missed the last check-in."

Ben leaned over the shoulder of Robert O'Neill, their computer expert. O'Neill was using satellite images to search the location where Manning should have been, as well as running a GPS trace. Everyone on the LASER team had a GPS homing beacon in their cell phone. Manning's cell was still in country, but not where it should be.

The itch at the back of Ben's neck said that his crappy day was about to get worse. And there was nothing he could do but wait for Manning to check in.

What the hell was going on?

"Sir, I think you should see this."

Ben turned to O'Neill, who was monitoring the cable news networks as well as watching all the satellite monitors. Ben leaned over his shoulder. Shannon Conner appeared on the screen, her blond hair windblown and her brown eyes more worried than usual.

Ben knew Shannon through Alex and Tory. They'd both gone to school with Shannon at Athena Academy. Shannon had the distinction of being the only student ever to be expelled from Athena. He knew that she and Tory didn't get along. Though Tory wouldn't say why, Ben had always suspected it went deeper than mere competitiveness.

"ABS News sources have learned that UBC

reporter Andrea Jancey, a UBC translator and a cameraman have been taken hostage in the small Middle Eastern country of Berzhaan. Here is the exclusive video that we've obtained."

Shannon's image faded to be replaced by a video feed that showed Andrea, Paul Manning—Ben's man—and Cobie McIntire.

The three said nothing, only held a copy of that day's newspaper underneath their faces to show the date. Andrea was a tall, curvy blonde. Normally she was perfectly put together but in the video her tailored suit was ripped and she had a bruise along the side of her face. Paul's nose was bleeding, and his cropped black hair looked matted on one side with blood or sweat. Cobie, a tall, lanky guy with shaggy brown hair, just looked shocked. The video went black and Shannon was once again back on the screen.

"ABS News will be following this story and will keep you up to date."

Ben tossed the headphones down and paced back to the command center. Well, now they knew why Manning hadn't checked in. "When was this video shot?"

Robert and Lewis both scrambled to get the information. Ben cursed under his breath. He had to contact his commanding officer and plan what to do next. Manning was part of Ben's team…more than that, he was a friend. Ben's gut said to go after him immediately.

But he couldn't make that type of decision without orders. He put a call in to his CO and set up an in-briefing with the field general in Berzhaan. Ben knew that their mission wouldn't change in essence—they still had to find those two Marine chopper pilots who'd gone down in the mountains. Now, they also had to retrieve Manning and the TV crew he'd been using as cover.

As soon as she realized that Andrea Jancey had been taken hostage, Tory Patton went into action. She phoned her boss and made an appointment to see him.

Tory had convinced Andrea to come to the United Broadcasting Company. She felt personally responsible for the young woman whom she'd been mentoring in the television news business. She'd steered Andrea away from risky assignments and trained the girl to keep a cool head. Now Andrea was in danger, and Tory needed details.

Andrea's field producer, Joan Simpson, was still in Suwan, the capital of Berzhaan. Tory spent ten minutes on the phone with her, ascertaining the situation and getting what information she could. She jotted notes on the paper in front of her, a quick list of facts plus the news that ABS had reported. That *Shannon Conner* had reported. Damn.

Next she put in a call to Jay Matthews, her favorite cameraman.

"What can I do for my favorite reporter?" Jay asked with an edge to his voice that hadn't been there before their time together in Puerto Isla nearly two years ago. Before he'd pushed her for a personal relationship and she'd had to turn him down. The assignment on which she'd met Ben.

He'd asked for a transfer overseas and had been covering the ongoing military action in the Middle East. She wanted him by her side, if she could convince Tyson to send her to Berzhaan. "Did you hear about Andrea and Cobie?"

"Yes, what have you heard?"

"Shannon was just on with a breaking story. I'm going to see Tyson in a few minutes."

"If you get him to send you, I'll work with you on this. I'll dig around and see what I can find for you until you get here. Even if they send someone else. Damn, I can't believe ABS broke the story on our own missing reporter."

"Pisses me off, too. Thanks, Jay."

"No problem, Patton."

She disconnected the call, turning to her computer. She sent an e-mail to Cathy Jackson in UBC research.

Cathy—
Please pull together whatever you can on Andrea Jancey and Cobie McIntire and their last known coordinates. Find out any information on who their contacts were and what story they were following. Thanks, Tory

She also placed a called to Yasmine Constanine to see if she would be amenable to anchoring the show while Tory was in the field. She then e-mailed her producer, Shawna Townsend, and ran the proposed idea past her. Shawna soon replied with the green light. Now all Tory had to do was get Tyson to go for it.

She camped in her boss's office for twenty minutes making small talk with Anita—Tyson Bedders's secretary—while they waited for him to return from a meeting. As soon as he saw Tory, he groaned.

"Not now, Patton."

"Yes, now, Tyson. I need to go to Berzhaan and find out what happened to Andrea."

"We're on it. You have a show now, and anchors don't go into the field."

It was the same argument he'd used to keep her from covering hurricanes last fall and from heading to London after a terrorist attack. To be honest, she was sick of being an anchor. Sure it had been her dream, but she had to admit that dream had been based on reaching a goal that had seemed far off more than on understanding what it entailed. "Then take me out of the anchor spot."

He rubbed the back of his neck. Tyson was a tall African-American man with one of the sharpest minds in the business. He was the kind of boss that most people dreamed of having, and Tory didn't like to put pressure on him.

She followed him into his corner office. "Okay, so what's the scoop? Why did ABS get the story before us? This is one of our people."

"Shannon Conner was already in Berzhaan and the terrorists sent the video to her."

"Well, it's an interesting move on their part, to take one of our reporters."

"Yes, it is. Did you hear their demands?" he asked.

"Not yet. As soon as I heard the news I started working on getting down there to find Andrea and Cobie."

"I haven't approved that yet, Patton."

"Tyson, I'm the only one you can send. I know Andrea, I trained her. I know the way she thinks. I'll find her."

"Tory, you asked for this promotion, your own

newsmagazine, and yet you're always in my office wanting me to send you back into the field."

She knew what he was saying. Understood that she wasn't fulfilling the commitment she'd made to Ty and the network when she'd said she'd take the anchor position. But anchoring just wasn't as exciting as she'd thought it would be, she craved the adrenaline rush that being in the field gave her. She missed the excitement and camaraderie of waiting at the assignment desk to see what kind of story she'd be given. She missed the unpredictability of always doing something new.

"What did they demand in exchange for the hostages? And who are 'they,' by the way?"

"The terrorists didn't name themselves. It's odd—no one knows if they're Q'rajn, or part of the Kemeni rebels, or some new group. They want a total U.S. pullout from the region in three weeks time."

"That's not even realistic. There's no way the government will go for that. They don't bargain with terrorists, anyway."

"We know."

"Come on, Ty. Let me go down there and see what I can find. I'm the best investigative reporter you have."

He rolled his eyes. "Every one of you thinks that. There's no ego like the investigative reporter ego."

She bit her lip, staying quiet. She knew her boss well enough to know that he'd give her a shot if she didn't push him into a position where it didn't look as if it were his decision.

"This has to be the last time you leave the anchor desk. Do you remember your latest contract negotiation, when you lobbied for this job? A show of your own where you could bring cutting-edge stories to the viewers at home?"

"I didn't realize that I'd be bringing them stories that *other* people researched, Tyson. That's not me. You know it's not."

"I know, Patton. That's why I cut you some slack usually, but this has to end."

She jumped up from her chair. "Of course, when I get back from Berzhaan, I'll stay put."

"I'm going to hold you to that."

She nodded, knowing she was going to have make a few changes to make that happen. To be happy with the choices she'd made.

"I've already started working out the details for my trip. I hope to get out of town tonight."

"You need to get your shots up-to-date. And don't tell me they are. I had Anita pull your file before I went to my meeting. You haven't even had your required yearly physical."

"Ty, that's a waste of time. I'm healthy has a horse."

"Whatever. No examination, no Berzhaan. And I'm not budging on this. Immunizations and yearly physicals are mandatory for all staff members going out of the country."

Tory added the exam to the growing list in her head of what needed to be done. She hated the time it would take. She needed to contact AA.gov to see if Andrea had been doing anything extra for them while she was in Berzhaan. Now Tory had to focus on a stupid physical. "I'm healthy, Tyson. You know I am. What if they can't get me in?"

He reached for his phone and hit the intercom button. "Anita?"

"Yes, Tyson?"

"Does Ms. Patton have a doctor's appointment this afternoon?" Tyson asked. He had a pen and pad of paper in one hand. He passed the pad to her.

"Yes, sir. With Dr. Waters in twenty minutes. She should leave now if she's going to be on time."

"Thanks, Anita. Do you have the address?"

Anita rattled it off and Tory wrote it down. She was going to really be pushing it to reach the doctor's office on time. Tyson disconnected the intercom and raised one eyebrow at her.

"Thanks, Ty."

He nodded. "Bring Andrea back and get the

story. We can't have our competition making us look like idiots."

She left his office and went back to her own, grabbing her purse and her cell phone. She saw that she had voice mail, a message from Ben. He sounded tired, and hearing his voice made her miss him.

She'd seen a photo of him in the *Daily Globe* with two British heiresses at a polo match. Despite the fact that his family knew they were dating, to the rest of the world, Ben had to appear to be the playboy he'd once been. It was the perfect cover for him. She understood. Knew the job he did was demanding and worthwhile. Her twinge of jealousy at seeing her man wrapped around two tall beauties wasn't something she should feel—but she did.

Voice mail wasn't the same as talking to him. She missed him, and she didn't like that. She wasn't used to depending on anyone else and a part of her resented the way she felt about Ben. The hold he had over her emotions unsettled her, because it was something she couldn't control.

But she didn't have time to think about Ben or their relationship. She had a meaty story to sink her teeth into. This story was going to be the kind of challenge she'd been longing for, after sitting behind the anchor desk and interviewing politicians and heads of state.

* * *

Russ Dorn felt alive for the first time since he'd received the news that his only son, Private First-Class Thomas Russell Dorn, had been killed in the line of duty in Berzhaan. The terrible weight that had pressed down on him every day, as he'd sat in front of his computer reading the newswire stories about the continuing effort to bring peace to an area that didn't want it and the climbing death toll, had fed his own anger and need to do something.

In an Internet chatroom he'd found other like-minded individuals who had also lost children in the Middle East. They'd formed a loosely organized group, at first to support one another. Over time, it had grown into an action group. Their mission was to prevent other parents from having to experience what they did.

They'd been to Washington, D.C., too many times and had come away frustrated. The death toll from the Middle East action continued to rise, and the grief of the parents continued to grow. Nothing short of serious action would stop the deaths.

The door opened and Larry Maxwell walked in wearing desert camouflage and an AK-47 slung over his shoulder.

"The package has been acquired," Dorn said. "We're set to meet the rest of the team in-country."

"Berzhaan. Damn. I never thought I'd leave the

3734622

U.S.A. again," Larry answered. "Well, this place looks good. We've got to move if we're going to make our rendezvous. My plane's waiting."

Larry had more money than God. He'd arranged the difficult parts of their transport, namely, getting in and out of countries with the hostages.

"Just wanted to be sure we had everything ready before we brought 'em here."

"This place is just as you said."

This place was empty, much like his life had become. Russ remembered that when Betty had been alive it had been a comfortable retreat. Not anymore.

Larry nodded. Both men walked through the room one more time before stepping outside. The desert was hot and dusty, different from places where he'd seen action when he'd been in the military years before. The desert terrain didn't even come close to resembling the jungles of Southeast Asia, but being with these other men and functioning together as a unit brought that memory into focus.

He rubbed the back of his neck and looked at the small hunting shack that he'd had on his property for more years than he could count. Larry went around back to double-check that area, and Russ fought against memories of the first time he'd brought Tommy out here. Damn. Sometimes he could still see his son on the ramshackle front porch, leaning against the beam and watching the sun rise over the great expanse of desert.

Betty had given the place little touches of home, a Marine Corps sun catcher in the window, pretty handwoven Navajo rugs on the floor. Russ hadn't been able to remove the reminders of his late wife. They were dusty and weathered with age, but he didn't care.

His mind still had a hard time understanding how he could have survived three tours in 'Nam but his son hadn't lasted a week on his first deployment. It wasn't right that Russ should live after facing fire so many times and young Tom didn't.

He shook off his grief and focused instead on the job he had to do now. He and Larry climbed into his old Ford pickup. The truck had seen better days, much like Russ himself. He drove unerringly over the desert where there was no track or road to speak of. Just a big barren empty landscape. A place that hid a million dangers. Poisonous snakes, plants, insects. Not one had ever harmed his son.

Russ felt tears burn at the back of his eyes and his anger grew as he approached the private landing strip. He had his doubts that this course of action was the right one but at the end of the day, sitting around and waiting for someone else to step in was too much.

Besides, if he sat alone in his house for one more

day, he was going to give in to the temptation to swallow the barrel of his old six-shooter. And Russ wasn't ready to give up his life yet. Not until he'd exhausted all avenues of getting the U.S. military out of Berzhaan. That wouldn't bring his boy back, and he knew it. But taking action, doing something constructive for a change, was what he needed to do to finally move past the mind-numbing routine of raising the American flag and then visiting his son's grave every day.

Chapter 2

Tory dialed Ben's cell number from the cab on her way to her doctor's appointment. She knew it was a longshot but since she knew that Ben was in the business of rescuing hostages, she hoped he'd be able to help with Andrea.

His phone rang only once before it was answered. "Forsythe."

Ben had a deep, sexy voice that she never quite got used to. It was hard to imagine the man she once thought of as a fluff-brained society boy turning her on just by saying her name, but it happened.

"Hey, it's me."

"Hello, me. Did you get my voice mail?"

She really missed him. But she'd never let him know. Knowing her own independent spirit, she'd fought to keep a distance between them, but lately it was growing harder. She wanted to feel his arms around her in the middle of the night.

"Yes, I did. I thought we talked about you not calling me *babe*."

"Must have slipped out. Are you calling to chew me out for that?"

"No, that's not why I'm calling."

"Why *are* you calling?" he asked.

She didn't know where he was or what he was doing. And at first, that hadn't bothered her, because her job was demanding and she couldn't really talk about it, either. But lately her mother had started to notice Ben's playboy-cover pictures, and she'd told Tory she didn't understand how the man she'd met last Christmas could be so into her daughter and still be seeing all those other women.

"Andrea Jancey has been taken hostage by some terrorists."

"I've heard."

"I'm going to Berzhaan to do some investigative reporting."

"Tory, don't come—don't go there. The country isn't stable."

"Neither was Puerto Isla, but I came out of there fine."

"Barely," he said.

She wasn't going to argue with him. "I have a job to do."

"I thought you were an anchor."

"I am. But Ty thought I was the best person for this story."

"I don't. It's dangerous."

"Good thing you're not my boss. Your job is no walk in the park, but you don't hear me telling you to stay home."

He sighed. She heard it over the connection and suspected he was running his hands through his thick, dark hair, something he always did when she frustrated him.

"I didn't call to fight with you," she said. "I want your help."

"With what?" She heard the caution in his voice.

"Finding Andrea. I thought maybe you could—"

"No. We don't get involved with civilians."

"But she's a friend, Ben. She was like my little sister at Athena. I mentored her, recommended her as UBC's Berzhaan correspondent."

"Babe, it's not your fault she was taken."

"I know that. Really I do, but she wouldn't be there if it weren't for me. I have to do what I can to help her."

"You're going to be stubborn about this, aren't you?"

"I don't think of it as stubborn," she said. It was

her job to get to the bottom of situations like Andrea's. To find out exactly where her friend was.

"Can you please just let this go?"

What exactly was he asking her? Even Ty, who wanted her in the anchor chair, understood why she needed to go after this story. And Ben, who supposedly knew her better than her boss, should understand. "No."

"Dammit, woman. Sometimes you make me crazy."

She could tell he was trying to get them back on track. Away from the fight they both were dancing around, but she wasn't ready to backpedal and say that everything was okay.

"Too bad."

"Tory…"

"I can't just let you blow this off like it means nothing. This is what my job is. I can't refuse assignments because you think they might be dangerous."

"That's not what I meant."

"You like my job as long as I stay in New York while you go jetting around the world. I'm not a slippers-and-martini-holding kind of woman."

"I know that."

"Then act like you understand what it means."

He said nothing for a moment and the cab pulled

to a stop in front of the doctor's office. She paid the driver and stepped onto the sidewalk.

"Listen, I've got to go."

"Babe…understanding your job isn't the problem. I have a hard time thinking of you in danger and me not being there to save you."

"I don't need you to save me." She'd spent her entire life proving that she didn't need anyone, afraid to let any person glimpse her vulnerabilities and insecurities. But she feared she needed Ben. He was the only man she'd ever really felt comfortable being herself around. The only man she'd let see the real Tory.

"But I need to. It's part of my makeup."

She understood that about Ben. She liked the fact that he did want to protect her. But that didn't mean she'd avoid danger to please him. "Get over it."

"I'm trying. I really am."

She knew that. She loved him for it. The way he fought against his own instincts because he knew that she didn't like it when he acted all macho. "Do you want to know my travel plans?"

"Hell."

"Is that a yes or no?"

She entered the building and took the elevator up to Dr. Waters's office. She signed in and found a seat in the corner, still waiting for Ben to respond.

"I guess that's a no."

He cursed savagely and she just waited, knowing he was fighting the same battle within himself that she always waged. They were both so strong-willed that their relationship wasn't smooth sailing for either of them.

"Ben?"

"It's not a freakin' no. Yes, tell me when you're leaving for Berzhaan. I'm going to be out of radio range for the next thirty-six hours. E-mail me your schedule."

"I will," she said, hating the feeling in her stomach that came from this new discontentment between them. It had been growing lately and she knew she was to blame. She wanted more from Ben but was afraid to ask for it. She could handle the toughest assignments, ask the hard questions of politicians and world leaders, but she had no idea how to ask Ben for what she wanted.

"Be safe," she said, quietly.

"You too," he said, and disconnected the call.

The capital city of Berzhaan wore its Russian influences well. Old and majestic, the architecture harkened back to a more civilized age. Ben rubbed the back of his neck as he ducked out of the busy foot traffic and into a familiar fast-food establishment where he was to meet his contact.

No matter what he might want to believe about a more graceful age, he knew that men like him had always been around and that fighting was something that had come naturally to this land in every age. There was something wild and untamed about the Middle East. Something that made even the most determined atheist sense there was a higher force at play in this land.

Ben ordered a Big Mac and fries from the attendant in perfect Russian. Most of the locals spoke Berzhaani, which was derived from Arabic, and Russian, after the country's long relationship with the former Communist nation. No matter where he was in the world, he could get a Big Mac, but there was still something a little weird about ordering one in Russian.

Ben found a table in the back of the restaurant and sat down. He opened the bag and prepared to wait for his contact. He'd just reached in to snag a fry when the clerk yelled out to stop him.

"Wait, sir. That is the wrong bag."

Ben pushed to his feet and handed the clerk the bag he'd been given. The new bag was slightly heavier and Ben glanced inside to see a small yellow capsule nestled in with his super-size fries.

"Thanks," he said to the clerk, and worked his way back out to the street. The last time he'd had fries had been with Tory in her apartment right before the start of this mission. They'd lain on the floor, watching another one of her favorite Tom Cruise movies and eating junk food.

He wanted to go back to New York, tie her to a chair and lock her in her apartment. He needed to know she was safe. She wouldn't understand it and he wasn't ever going to let her know it, but she made what he did worthwhile. Knowing that she was safe while he saved the world, or at least a small portion of it, made it easier for him to sleep at night. And he didn't want her anywhere near Berzhaan.

The Kemeni rebels had scattered after their defeat and the death of their leader Tafiq Ashurbeyli, during their takeover of Suwan's capitol building last February, but they were still out there. The last thing Ben wanted was for Tory to come here and start poking around.

The woman had a real talent for finding the truth and she never stopped once she was on the trail of a story. Should he have told her he'd be going after Andrea? Would she have listened to him and stayed in Manhattan? He doubted it.

He pocketed the capsule and blended into the throng of people on the street. He wanted to examine the information he'd been given, but he knew he couldn't out here.

A late model car pulled to a stop next to him. Ben identified Salvo and slid into the car. Salvo pulled away from the curb.

"How'd it go?"

"Smooth."

"Does anything ever not go smoothly for you?"

He thought of Tory and the constant frustration he felt at not being able to get through to her. He thought of his sister and the way she treated him as if he were letting down the family name with his globe-trotting ways. And his mother, who was disappointed that he still hadn't found himself an heiress and settled down. His personal life was one constantly changing mess.

"Yes. But only temporarily," Ben said. He had an image to keep up, especially around his men.

He palmed open the capsule and removed a tiny microdisc, passing it to O'Neill, who sat in the backseat. His small laptop computer was up and running, receiving information and dissecting it.

"This should be the coordinates of the rebel camp. Plug those in with Manning's last known location and the coordinates of the downed chopper."

"I'll have a location for you in a minute. I thought that the Kemenis disbanded after their attempt to take over Suwan last year."

"For the most part they did, but the survivors are still ready to fight."

"Any idea who the leader of the new movement is?" O'Neill asked.

Ben didn't take his eyes off the terrain. "That's not our mission, O'Neill."

"It'd be nice to have the upper hand a time or two. Remember that FUBAR mission on Puerto Isla?" O'Neill asked.

"Hell, yes. What a fuckup," Salvo said. "But Slick here got us through with no problems."

"That's what they pay me for," Ben said.

They left Suwan, heading south out of town. The lights of the city dropped away behind them as they rode out into the barren landscape. The military unit they were entrenched with was about thirty miles away in the foothills.

The night closed in around them as they sped along the deserted highway. O'Neill worked on his computer in the backseat while Ben monitored the radio for updates. They'd had an in-briefing earlier in the day and they were still a go on retrieving the marines. The ROEs—rules of engagement—were to stay focused on getting the Marines out, to expect some hostile fire and to engage only if necessary. The CO didn't expect them to sustain any causalities.

Suddenly a round of gunfire ripped through the

night. Salvo cursed and floored the gas pedal and Ben pulled his firearm and returned fire. O'Neill did the same out of the other window.

The Kemeni rebels had been driven out of Suwan, but they still patrolled the roads and sometimes shot at cars to make their presence felt. This time they'd get a little more than they bargained for. Ben prayed they'd back off now that he and his men were returning fire. Last week, a group of missionaries had nearly been taken hostage when they'd stopped to change a tire, and Ben and his men couldn't afford to talk nice to keep their own freedom. It was kill or be killed.

The car sputtered. Salvo kept his foot on the gas, but they all heard the whine that signaled the radiator had been hit.

"We'll dump the car and continue on foot," Ben said.

"Yes, sir."

Salvo steered them onto the shoulder and all three men got out of the car. The enemy gunfire had ceased, but the vehicle was DOA.

They fell into an easy formation, Salvo and Ben standing guard while O'Neill packed up his computer. They shot the gas tank and let the car burn, careful to stay out of the light cast by the flames. The car was registered to an attaché at the U.S. Military listening station. They didn't need for it to be identified until the LASER team was out of country. This way the car could be reported as stolen.

"Ready to roll, sir."

"Let's move out."

As they moved across the desert, all that Ben heard was a series of clicks on the radio. He'd been in a hundred situations like this one, but for the first time, as they made their way on foot back to the military base, he felt a churning in his gut that wasn't excitement.

A churning that said that a man could die out here and his family might never find out what had happened to him. A churning that said maybe his luck was finally running out now that he had someone to live for.

Tory got off the plane in Germany for a short layover, the news from her doctor's appointment still churning through her head. Her cell phone beeped as soon as she turned it on. She glanced at the caller ID. Her mother seemed to have a built-in radar to know when to call.

Tory had sent her an e-mail saying she was leaving on assignment but not detailing what she was doing. Her parents tended to worry whenever she left New York. And right now she had news she just didn't want to spill to her parents yet.

"Hi, Mom."

"Hey, sweetie. Dad and I wanted to invite you to come down to the ranch for the Fourth. Derrick and his family are going to be here."

"Just me?" she asked.

"Are you still with Ben?"

Tory sighed, not sure she'd ever really make her mother understand the complexities of that relationship. And not knowing how to tell her it had just gotten a lot more complex. "Yes, I am."

"Of course we'd love it if he came with you," Charlotte Patton said.

She loved the way her mom covered her own dislike of Ben by making it sound as if he'd be welcome. Tory had a sudden picture of Derrick and her dad taking Ben out to a remote area of the ranch and talking to him about commitment. She smiled to herself. There was something to be said for being the baby of the family and being surrounded by their love. *Baby.* Oh lord.

"We can't make it. I'm on my way to Berzhaan to cover a story."

"I knew it was someplace dangerous. As soon as I read that e-mail I said to Dad, look at the way she didn't say where she was going."

"Mom, it's not dangerous. It's a foreign assignment. The same as when I've been to Ireland or London."

"It is not the same, Victoria. A news crew was taken hostage there."

"That's why I'm going. I'll e-mail you when I have a chance."

"Be careful, Tory."

"I will." *If you only knew....* But this wasn't the time.

"Tory?"

"Yes?"

"I…I'm sorry I asked about Ben like that."

"Mom, it's okay. I understand why you did."

"Love you, honey."

"Love you, too."

She hung up the phone and entered the VIP waiting room. She powered up her laptop and focused on work, doing what research she could before she got to Suwan.

She tried to concentrate but her mind was filled with the news she'd gotten at the doctor's office.

She was pregnant.

She'd tried to put it from her mind. It wasn't as if she felt any different today than she had yesterday. She looked the same, had even spent precious minutes in front of her bedroom mirror trying to see some physical evidence of the baby that was inside her, but there wasn't anything yet.

She'd almost told her mom, but how was she going to explain her pregnancy when she hadn't had a chance to talk it over with Ben? And given her mom's concerns about the relationship, about Ben's

picture always appearing in magazines and news-
papers with gorgeous women….

She checked her e-mail and saw she had one from
Alex.

I can't get Ben to call me back, are you two going
to be around on the weekend of Fourth? We want
to see you.

Tory rubbed her head where she felt the begin-
nings of a bad headache. She and Ben both came
from families who were tight and close, she thought.
They shared that kind of upbringing and yet there
was a part of both them that liked to be alone.

D.C. was closer than Florida and Ben's family
wouldn't ask uncomfortable questions. Plus, lately,
she suspected that Alex had realized there was more
to Ben's job than met the eye.

She swallowed hard. She was never really going
to be alone again. She'd have a child with her for the
rest of her days. *A child.*

The words echoed in her head and she felt her
entire world spinning out of control. The world that
she'd always kept carefully ordered was being filled
with chaos.

*Get hold of yourself, Patton. You're an Athena grad,
not some average wimp.* She took a deep breath and

pulled her Blackberry PDA/cellular phone from her pocket to check Ben's calendar. He was supposed to be back in the country on Monday. The Fourth was on Friday so they might be able to see the Forsythe family.

But Tory wasn't sure that she'd be back from Berzhaan by then. True, it was seven days away, but the timing might be too close.

Deep inside she knew she was being a coward, afraid to face Alex knowing that she was pregnant with Ben's child. Afraid to be at a family gathering and know she was carrying the great-grandchild that patriarch Charles Forsythe craved. Afraid that she was going to have to come clean before she was ready to.

She e-mailed Alex a quick note cautioning her that they might not make it. She mentioned Andrea and the kidnapping, which Alex had undoubtedly heard about by now, and the fact that she was on her way to Berzhaan.

She e-mailed the three UBC field producers in Berzhaan with the information she'd pulled together so far and asked them to forward anything they had from Andrea. A producer hadn't been assigned to Tory yet. She hoped that she'd get Joan Simpson, who'd worked directly with Andrea. At the very least she wanted to talk to the woman.

Tory was booked into the same hotel that Andrea

had stayed in and planned to start looking for clues to her friend's whereabouts there.

Her phone rang again. "Patton."

"It's Jay. I've spent all day roaming around Suwan looking for any locals who might have seen Andrea or know what story she's been following."

"Did you find any?" she asked, pulling out her notepad to take notes.

"One guy, but I'm not positive he didn't have Andrea and Shannon confused. He said he saw *the blond TV woman* yesterday. I'm going to see if I can find anyone to corroborate that."

What if Shannon had been the target? What if Andrea had been taken by mistake? Both women were similar in height and build. Tory made a note to find out what she could about Shannon and her reporting from Suwan.

"That's something. Can you check out where she was and see what she was asking about? Maybe try to find a more reliable source? I'll be there shortly and I'm going to want to roll as soon as I hit the ground. I've been in touch with the producers and they said Andrea had a hot tip about some sort of rescue mission. Did you get a lead on anything like that?"

"Not a word, but I spoke only to locals. I didn't think there were any hostages until Andrea and crew got nabbed."

"Me either. I'll start digging on this end and see what I can find."

"Sounds good. I'll meet you at your hotel later."

She turned her attention back to her computer and started looking through files, searching the wire and the databases she had access to.

Thirty minutes later she found what she was looking for. A unit of Marines had gone down in the mountains of Berzhaan when their helicopter was hit by enemy fire. Four men were rescued but two were missing.

She had a tingling in her stomach that she couldn't ignore. Ben was in Berzhaan. Was he close to Suwan? Had he seen Andrea? Damn him for being so cool on the phone when she'd mentioned the incident.

What kind of relationship did they have?

She understood the need for secrecy. She wouldn't betray him. When was he going to start trusting her?

Chapter 3

Russ Dorn didn't like the heat in Berzhaan. It hung in the air in oppressive waves, making a man struggle to breathe. Their contact, a young Berzhaani named Momar, had brought robes for all of his team.

Russ shifted in his djellaba, not comfortable with the fabric draping over his camouflage. But he knew the importance of blending in. He stopped at the back of the large open-air market and rubbed some dirt into his graying beard to darken it.

He purchased enough kaffiyeh for all the men. He spoke in Barzhaani, which he'd learned through deep immersion at home, playing only the Suwan national television station and listening to tapes from Berzhaan.

He'd always had a gift for languages and he'd picked up Berzhaani easily, brushing up on his Russian as well. The language was now a part of him and as he stood in the marketplace letting the sounds flow over him, he felt himself becoming more Berzhaani. He felt it seep into his pores and he was ready for action.

Larry waited in a small alleyway with Jake Brittan and Rodney Petri, two other fathers who'd joined the group. This was Russ's elite inner militia. Men who knew how to act in a combat situation and weren't afraid of the risks. Frankly, the ROE on this mission meant there'd be casualties and Russ knew each of the men was unafraid to give his life for the cause.

They donned the kaffiyeh headgear and Russ thought they did a good job of looking like men of Islam.

"Do you have the address for us?" Russ asked Rodney.

"It's on Sovetski—the name has been changed to something Berzhaani, but the locals still call it Sovetski. Its two klicks from the embassy in a small residential neighborhood. I've programmed the GPS coordinates into your devices."

Russ nodded at Rodney. "We'll meet there at sunset. Larry and I are going to secure local transport back to the plane. You two make sure we have the carpets needed to get our package out of Berzhaan."

Rodney and Jake departed and Larry fiddled with his backpack for a minute before handing Russ a Stechkin APS Russian automatic handgun. Russ checked the gun and the clip. He took an extra ammo clip from Larry and tucked it into the back of his pants for easy access.

"You sure about this?" Larry asked. "Once we go in there, we can't turn back."

Russ looked the man in the eyes. Larry had been his buddy for more than twenty years and he didn't want him chickening out before the mission barely got started. This was what too many years and too much grief did to a man. There was a time when Larry would have taken all of Berzhaan with an AK-47 and a few grenades.

"Yes. Are you?" Russ asked, holding his gun easily at his side. Casually he removed the kaffiyeh from his head and folded the scarflike garment into the right size and density for a silencer.

Larry turned his back to Russ and Russ lifted the gun and the cloth. Larry glanced over his shoulder at Russ, eyes widening and hands coming up in an "I surrender" gesture.

Larry took a step back. "Yeah, man. I'm sure. I

want our kids back home where they belong, not in this godforsaken place."

Russ continued to stare at Larry until beads of sweat dotted Larry's forehead. Then he lowered his gun, tucking it into the large pocket in the middle of the djellaba. "Then let's make sure they go home."

Larry nodded. Russ retied his kaffiyeh and led the way out of the alley. They both were careful to blend in with the people on the street. He'd have to keep a close eye on Larry in case he decided he wanted out of the mission.

Both men moved through the street with the ease of pros used to blending in. They were both hunters, well aware of how to keep their prey from becoming aware of them.

Russ felt a surge of adrenaline. There was something to be said about being on a mission with his comrades at his side. They meandered through the city, which had seen too much fighting in recent years. It showed. Some neighborhoods were still intact but others were shelled-out hulls that used to house families that were probably dead.

Russ felt his determination to make this mission a success harden as they arrived on Sovetski and the house that Jake had indicated. The building reminded Russ of some of the pictures he'd seen of Moscow.

Jake and Rodney waited on the first floor landing of the older apartment building. The Kemeni soldiers they'd hired to obtain their package waited upstairs. Russ didn't want trouble but he was prepared for it. These men had been bought once and could just as easily have sold them out.

"We go in hard."

"Affirmative."

All the men pulled their weapons as they slowly made their way up the stairs.

They entered the building and moved in single-file formation up the stairs. They were dark and dirty and smelled of rotting trash and urine.

Jake moved to the front and Russ covered him as the other man knocked on the third door.

"I'm here to see Uncle Fred," Jake said in Russian.

"He's still recovering from the car accident, he'll be glad for the company," a voice answered from behind the door.

A few seconds later the door opened inward and the men filed in, all of them keeping their weapons drawn.

"I am Jamal, welcome to my home."

"Where's the package?" Russ asked, still in Russian. He wasn't here to make friends. They were on a short clock and needed to get in and out as quickly as possible.

"In a room in the back," Jamal said.

Russ started toward the room. "Is there a guard in the room?"

"Two of my men." Jamal edged down the hallway toward a closed door.

"Tell them to stand down," Russ ordered.

Jamal switched to Berzhaani, calling out, "The men are here and they are armed."

"You first, Jamal."

Russ gestured with his gun and Jamal went into the room. Two men sat at a card table, weapons in close range. On the floor were the hostages. All three of them neatly bound, gagged and unconscious. Drugged, as ordered.

They all looked so young, Russ thought, especially the girl. Just like Tommy had. This girl could have been one of his girlfriends.

Russ carefully controlled his burning anger with the kidnappers—they were supposed to take that annoying sensationalist reporter, Shannon Conner, and give the hostage tape to this woman, Andrea something. Shannon was better known—her kidnapping would have put even more pressure on the White House. Just because the opposite had worked out didn't mean he could let the men off the hook for their mistake. But for now, Russ would work with what he had. As every good soldier did.

The White House should be ashamed of the way it kept the military here in Berzhaan now that the Kemenis were not a threat. If they'd pulled the military back home, then this young woman and two men wouldn't be here now. They'd be safe at home.

"Where's the video camera?" he asked Jamal, this time in Berzhaani.

"In the corner."

"Set it up. We want to make one more tape before we leave."

The lobby of the Sheraton Suwan hotel was filled with reporters, and Tory kept an eye out for Shannon Conner. She had a history with the newsperson from the rival ABS network. For some reason Tory couldn't explain, she and Shannon had never gotten along—not even before Tory had exposed Shannon in the scheme that had caused Shannon to be expelled from Athena Academy.

More than 15 years later, Shannon still held a grudge. She'd slept with Tory's last boyfriend, Perry Jacobs, and almost gotten Tory killed on Puerto Isla in Central America.

Tory was leery of seeing Shannon, yet at the same time she wanted to know where the newswoman had been. Just in case Andrea had been nabbed by mistake.

"Tory Patton?"

Tory pivoted toward the voice. "Yes?"

"Dash McNamara. I'll be your segment producer while you're in Suwan. Welcome."

She shook Dash's hand. "Thanks. I'm all checked in. I think we're supposed to be reporting live in less than forty minutes."

"You're correct. I've already scouted a few locations for the remote broadcast that are away from the hotel. Most of the networks do a nightly broadcast from the balcony overlooking the city, but I know you like to be different."

Tory smiled at him, impressed that he'd done his research. "What can I say? I don't like to be part of the crowd."

"You never could be," he said, leading her through the people in the lobby. Jay lounged against the wall, cigarette in one hand, camera bag in the other. Next to him was a kid who looked too young to be working in their business.

"I believe you know Jay Matthews. And this is Sal Martini, my PA."

Tory hugged Jay, glad to see her old friend here. He smelled of cigarettes and coffee. The scent overpowered her for a minute and she battled a wave of nausea. Damn, she'd almost forgotten about her pregnancy until her stomach reminded her. Jay held her longer than he should have, but it had been a long time since they'd seen each other, so she didn't mind.

She shook Sal's hand.

"It's a pleasure to meet you, Ms. Patton," Sal said. "If you need anything just let me know."

"If you give Sal your bag and laptop, he can store them until we return to the hotel," Dash said.

Tory handed over her laptop bag and her suitcase but kept the big messenger-style bag that she always carried. She had notes and notepads in there, pens and minirecorders. Everything she needed to work.

She followed the men out of the hotel into the steamy June day.

A small Renault was parked in the lot to the side of the building. She noticed crumbling mortar and cracks in the wall. The city of Berzhaan was in desperate need of rebuilding.

"Were you working with Andrea?" she asked Dash.

"Not directly, but I produced one of her segments. On the day she disappeared, she left to scout an area for the evening report and never returned."

"What was she covering?" Tory asked as Jay held open the door to the car for her. She gestured for him to climb in the backseat. He winked at her as he did so.

Dash didn't answer. He got behind the wheel, started the car and drove toward the east side of the city.

"What was Andrea working on, Dash?" she asked again once they were on the highway leading down toward the port.

"The story of some U.S. Marines who have been missing for almost a week. The rest of the unit was rescued from the mountains on the border between Berzhaan and Afghanistan, but two men are still missing."

"Was Andrea close to finding out if they were alive?" Tory asked. She pulled her notebook out and started making notes. She thought better on paper.

"Not the last time we spoke. She said she was stopping in a local neighborhood to check a lead, then she and the crew were headed to the foothills of the mountains to give her report from there. Her cameraman, Cobie McIntire, was with her, and a translator."

"Did she have her Blackberry with her?" Tory asked, knowing that the network made sure to track all their foreign correspondents with a GPS unit in their phones.

"Yes, she did. We checked that first thing. The unit has been destroyed, but we have the times and coordinates of her final movements."

Tory's heart clenched in fear for her young

friend. As an Athena graduate, Andrea knew how to handle herself in the real world. But this wasn't an everyday situation.

Dash eased the car onto the shoulder and gestured toward the Caspian Sea. "This is one of the locations I found. There's an outcropping that's big enough for you and Jay to stand on and shoot."

Tory looked at the sea. She didn't even know what she was going to say tonight. "I need to talk to officials and get up-to-the-minute information."

"How would you like an on-air interview with the lead investigator from the Berzhaani police?"

"I'd love it. Where are we meeting him?"

"Right here, in about ten minutes," Jay said. "Stop teasing her, Dash, and give her the stuff we gathered today."

Dash handed her a small sheaf of papers. She started reading them, effortlessly committing the facts to memory.

Jay leaned forward. "I'm getting out," he said. "I want to double-check the area where we're shooting."

Tory got out of the car as well and leaned against the hood, reading the report that had been filed and the few clues the police had uncovered. Shortly after the kidnapping, the vehicle Andrea and her crew had been driving had been used for a suicide bombing at a military checkpoint at one of the border crossings into Afghanistan.

She prayed that Andrea was still alive, and hoped her friend hadn't been in the trunk of the car that been used as a weapon against Berzhaan.

"Do we know if the car blew up after the tape was shot showing them alive?"

"Not yet. We obtained a copy of the tape and the guys in editing have been analyzing it to ensure its validity."

Tory closed her eyes and searched for the story she'd tell on the news. The facts were foggy. No one knew too much. She had a number of pointed questions for the lead detective on the case. "Is anyone from the American embassy involved in the investigation?"

"Yes, but they won't talk to us on air or off."

"CIA?"

"I'm not sure. We're poking around where we can, but they warned us strongly to back off."

"I'll see what I can come up with," Tory said. She planned to track down Ben and find out exactly what was going on with Andrea, her crew and the two missing Marines. There was definitely more here then met the eye.

After the shoot, Tory left Jay and Dash in the hotel lobby and went to look for Joan Simpson, Andrea's producer.

The police investigator had put a nice spin on the story, telling Tory on-camera that the investigation showed definite progress and off camera that he had men undercover following leads.

Jay had chain-smoked during the ride back and Tory felt a little sick. Since smoke had never bothered her before, she had to believe that her pregnancy was responsible. She was barely six weeks along, and already the pregnancy was affecting her life.

She really hated feeling so out of control. After she talked to Joan, she was going on the Internet to research pregnancy. She'd find a way to manage this the same way she did everything else.

She was standing against one of the columns breathing in the clean air when she saw Joan. The tall brunette was a few years older than Tory but looked as if she'd aged at least ten years since Tory had seen her nine months earlier.

Joan sat in the corner of the bar, a glass of rye whiskey on the table in front of her. No sissy girly drinks for Joan, who'd started in the sports department and proved herself to be one of the guys.

Tory pulled the strap of her purse higher on her shoulder and approached Joan.

"Can I join you?" Tory asked.

Joan glanced up. "Sure, Tory. What's up?"

"I wanted to talk to you about Andrea and Cobie and their translator, do you mind?"

"Not at all. I keep thinking about them. Why didn't I see the danger before I sent them out?"

"No one could have predicted this."

"True, but that doesn't make sleeping at night any easier." Joan took a sip of her whiskey. "What do you want to know?"

"Where she'd been the last few days and what stories she was following."

"Well, she did all her live reports just outside the city in the desert region. Do you have a map?"

Tory pulled one out of her bag and set it on the table. Joan took the pen from Tory and marked the spot. "The station has a few cars in the motor pool— see Stan and he'll give you something to drive if you decide to go."

Tory nodded. Since Andrea and her crew had frequented that spot, the hostage takers could have predicted when she'd arrive and who would be with her.

"Next I'd look for a woman named Alaleh. She works in the open-air market, right here," Joan said, marking another spot on the map. "She's a rug merchant's wife. Alaleh has been very outspoken on the way women are treated here despite the American influences. She might be able to help you, but you can't see her until tomorrow morning."

Tory remembered that Andrea had done several stories on that topic. Because of the nature of the demands from the people holding her and the others hostage, Tory feared that America's influence over women in this region might have instigated the kidnapers going after Andrea.

"Is that it?"

"No, there's one more spot. Here." Joan marked an area a distance from Suwan near the mountain range that bordered Afghanistan. "This is near the insurgent camp in the mountains where we suspect the Marines are being held."

Tory stared at the map. "I called the press office for the Marine Corps to get some additional information from them, but they only referred to what they'd said in their press release."

"Andrea talked to someone else, I don't know who. The station had me box up all her notes and personal things. They're in the news suite—do you want to see them?"

"Yes," Tory said, and Joan finished her whiskey and led the way out of the bar.

"Do you think Andrea and Shannon Conner look similar?" Tory asked, advancing the theory that had been bothering her since Jay's comment about the blond reporter.

Joan stopped. "You know, they do. I never really thought about it before."

"Someone made a comment to Jay about the blond reporter, which got me thinking. Shannon and I aren't really close enough for me to ask her what she's been working on...."

"I'll see what I can find out. Will you be in the hotel?"

"No, I'm going out after this. You can always reach me on my cell."

The news suite was actually a quarter of the ballroom with partition doors around it to separate UBC from the other news networks. In a small, dark corner with pipe and drape surrounding it was the editing suite.

"Andrea's stuff is over here."

Joan led Tory to a small table that had a computer on it. A cardboard box lay on the floor under the table. "You can use this area while you're here."

Tory nodded to Joan and sat down in Andrea's chair. Joan drifted off to talk to some others in the newsroom, and Tory let the sounds drift away until the conversations became background music. She turned on Andrea's computer and booted it up.

She was tired. If only she could leave this for morning...but the terrorists who'd taken Andrea and her crew had only given the U.S. a few days to take action, and Tory didn't want to waste any of that limited window of opportunity.

She dug around in the box, hoping to find something that would give her a lead. She sat up when the LAN log-in screen popped up.

"Joan?" she called across the crowd. "Do you know Andrea's log-in?"

Joan walked back toward her. "I had the IT guys reset it. It's AJancey for log-in, UBCBERZ for password."

Tory typed it in. While the computer loaded Andrea's page, she pulled out a small stack of manila file folders. None of them were labeled. Inside one, she found the notes for the stories Andrea had filed for Tory's show, *A Closer Look.* They included interviews with Alaleh and a small group of women.

Tory put that file aside to take with her tomorrow when she tracked down Alaleh. She should be able to recognize the woman.

The next folder had clippings from the AP and Reuters on the Marine Huey that was shot down. She skimmed them but found nothing new in the press articles and no notes from Andrea.

She opened the Outlook e-mail program and read through Andrea's recent messages. The list had several familiar e-mail addresses and one surprising one. She didn't know that Andrea had started working for AA.gov.

Tory opened that e-mail with a feeling of trepidation. The message was brief and coded but Tory was familiar with the codes used by AA.gov, since she worked as a courier for the agency herself.

Andrea had been working on an assignment for the agency when she'd been taken hostage.

Chapter 4

The night air was cool and Ben sank deeper into his cover waiting for the signal from O'Neill. They'd retrieved the Marines from the Kemeni rebel camp high in the mountains and were now on their way back to the military base in the desert. Both of the Marines were severely injured and Velosi, the LASER team's medic, had stabilized them. They awaited retrieval by Huey in less than five minutes.

The back of Ben's neck itched and he had that feeling in his gut that everything was about to go to hell. He checked in with his men again and they were all okay. Dammit, what was bothering him?

The Huey landed and they loaded both Marines onto the chopper. He and his men stayed behind. He radioed his CO that their mission was complete and requested permission to start on the retrieval of Manning and the news crew. He got the go-ahead.

"We're green on our second mission," Ben said, rejoining his men in the chow hall on the desert base. His guys, all wearing desert camo and T-shirts, were sitting at a table for eight. Ben took his seat but there was still one spot that was empty, and they all were aware of the man who was missing.

"About damn time," L. J. Potchicki said. L.J. was the team's sniper and he held his weapons with an ease that made the rest of them look as if it was their first time holding a firearm. It almost seemed that the weapon was an extension of the man.

Next to him was Marshall George, or Georgie, as he was known. Georgie was Potchicki's spotter and the two men were close. They worked together day in and day out, as did the rest of the team, but they also drilled as a two-man unit, watching each other's back and trusting each other as they did no one else.

"Georgie and I have already restocked on ammo for the team. We're ready for anything we encounter."

Ben put his hand on Potchicki's shoulder. In Potchicki-speak, "anything they encountered" meant everything short of a nuclear attack. And even then

Ben wasn't too sure the sniper wasn't prepared. "O'Neill, what'd you find out? Anything new?"

"One of our guys traced the network satellite van to a location just outside the city," O'Neill said without glancing up from the computer in front of him.

"Did you confirm?" Ben asked, mentally compiling a picture of his team's readiness. They fairly vibrated with the need to be moving.

"Yes."

Ben nodded. "Then we'll start there. Somewhere between Manning's last GPS reading and the news van."

"His last reading was in the Berzhaan capital," Salvo said. "I've got a contact who's working on known terrorist hideouts within Suwan."

"How reliable is this source?" Ben asked. "Have you used him before?"

"Well, I bought him, so I guess we can trust him as far as what I paid. He's a Kemeni who's got no love for the U.S."

Berzhaan was in a dangerous position, with so many leaderless rebels in the land. The U.S. soldiers weren't the favored sons here, but then that was true of just about every country they traveled to.

"I say we take the little bastard with us and if his intel is wrong…"

Ben shook his head. The comment showed that the men were tense, but not in a nervous way. They were ready for action. They wanted their missing comrade back. Rescuing airmen was their job but rescuing one of their own—that was personal.

He left the men and went outside for a few minutes alone. Until Tory, he hadn't really thought much about the fact that he essentially did a young man's job. A job for the type of man who had nothing to lose and thought he'd never die. But Ben's thinking had changed somewhere over the last year and he wasn't sure he liked it.

Sure he liked what he had with Tory. But she wasn't the kind of woman he'd always pictured himself settling down with. For one thing, she didn't listen worth a damn. For another, she wasn't content to just be a wife. If she had been, he'd have asked her to marry him already. But as it was, he wasn't sure where they stood and he already sensed he was more attached to her than she was to him.

"Ben?"

"Yes, Velosi?" Ben asked. Each man had EMT training, but Carmine Velosi was their designated medic. The man had calm hands during the most intense firefight.

"Just wanted to check on that scrape you sustained as we were pulling out."

"It's fine. I bandaged it myself when we got back."

"You sure?" Velosi asked, but Ben knew that the medic had something other than the injury on his mind.

"I'm not going to lose my arm. What's up?"

"Wanted to let you know I put in for a transfer to headquarters."

Ben was surprised. "Thanks for the notice. I'd have sworn you were a lifer."

Velosi cleared his throat and moved a few feet away from Ben, glancing toward the horizon. "Abby's pregnant and she wants me closer to home."

Family. Ben understood family and the obligations that came with it more than the next man.

"Ben?"

"A man's gotta do what he can to keep his woman happy." Ben wasn't sure he believed that giving up the life he'd chosen was the right answer.

"Yeah, man. I'll be glad to get moving so I don't have to think anymore."

Ben clapped Velosi on the shoulder as the other men filed out of the chow tent. Ben held himself back. He needed to be in the center of the action, pumping his men up, but his head wasn't in the mission. It was with a certain petite anchorwoman who had the singular ability to distract him and make him crazy.

Why did she have such a hold over him? He'd

avoided thinking about it for so long, but lately he couldn't set his feelings aside. Something had changed between the two of them. Changed for the better, to make them both more tightly bonded, but at the same time that meant he had to give something up.

Would he be like Velosi, trading action and the thrill of pitting himself against an unknown enemy to sit at a desk and analyze data? Could he live like that? Would Tory want him to?

He shook his head and forced his mind back to the mission and away from a woman who messed with his job. Tonight they'd find Manning and rescue the UBC reporter and her cameraman or die trying.

Once again, he confronted the fact that he had someone to live for. Dying wasn't an option he wanted to explore.

Tory watched the second tape of the hostages four times before she got up and left the newsroom. She felt helpless when she saw her friend bound and gagged. She pushed past feelings of rage and started to break down the scene she'd just witnessed.

Dash and Jay came out after her. Jay lit up a cigarette and leaned back against the building, his long, lean frame reminiscent of the old Marlboro commercials of her youth.

"We need to get ready for your broadcast," Dash said.

"Jay, can you put that cigarette out?" Tory asked. She couldn't concentrate on her job and on keeping the nausea at bay at the same time.

He dropped the cigarette and stubbed it out with the toe of his boot.

"Thanks. Jay and I drove out toward the mountains earlier today and there was nothing there to indicate that Andrea or the crew had been there in the last few days."

"Makes sense. The car was found closer to the city limits," Dash said.

"Just eliminating all possibilities," Tory said. She was a thorough investigator who left nothing to chance. "Was anything odd about that tape we just saw?"

"I couldn't look past seeing them trapped like that," Dash said. "Let's go have another glance at it. Editing is making a loop of it and the first tape for us to run on your show tonight."

Back inside the newsroom they all leaned over the monitor until Dash was called away.

"Since when does smoking bother you?" Jay asked.

She glanced at him. They were leaning down to view

the monitor, pressed almost shoulder-to-shoulder. Jay's eyes were brilliant gray and hard as diamonds.

"Since…" Jay couldn't be the first person she told she was pregnant. "I have a bit of a headache and I thought it was the smoke."

He gave her a sardonic shrug and then turned back to the monitor. She wasn't a liar by nature and making up a story now felt wrong. She pushed that thought aside, focusing instead on Andrea.

"Look at the light pattern," Jay said.

"Late afternoon?"

"Or early evening."

"Clearly they're inside a building," she said. "Do you recognize the architecture? Is this reminiscent of Suwan?"

"Actually, I think it is. The light isn't the unfiltered brightness of the desert." As a cameraman, Jay understood light better than Tory did. She listened to him as he spoke more to himself than to her.

"The light is filtering through the windows. This is different than the first tape. Definitely not a desert landscape but subdued, like the afternoon lighting in Manhattan. Dispersed through the tall buildings and reflected off of skyscrapers."

"So they're in the city?"

"I can't be one hundred percent sure, but my gut says yes. A city anyway."

"I'll trust your gut."

"Tory, are you doing your broadcast from the same location as last night?"

"No. I want to use the marketplace as a backdrop. I interviewed Alaleh today about the women's vote and rights now that the city is supposedly out of the hands of the rebels."

Dash nodded. Earlier they'd discussed focusing her reports on something other than Andrea until they had a solid lead they could use. But the new film footage gave her something to discuss. "I'll lead with the hostage tape and then we can move on to the Alaleh piece."

"Good," Dash said, nodding to her. He was already moving through the newsroom. Tory stepped over to her computer to jot down her notes for the broadcast—the observations she'd made since she'd been in Suwan.

She typed them up and printed them out. There'd be no TelePrompTer at her broadcast location. Dash was still working with the editors to get both tapes ready for her show. She had a few minutes to check e-mail.

She was waiting for some response from AA.gov. There wasn't a message from them, but there was one from Alex.

We've got you and Ben down as a definite maybe for the Fourth. I hope you make it because I need to talk to you about that blackmailer, A, who uses a spider as a symbol. Sam and I have noticed this initial coming up in investigations connected to Athena Academy. Can you dig around and see what you can find?

A...spider. Tory remembered, Arachne was a Greek spider goddess who was in charge of weaving the web of fate. She was also an enemy of the goddess Athena. Could A stand for Arachne? Sounded as if they had someone with a god complex out there.

Alex had recently solved the decade-old, cold case murder of Athena Academy founder Marion Gracelyn. Alex and Marion's daughter, Allison, had learned Marion was being blackmailed by someone who signed letters with an A. "A" had threatened Marion with exposing another dear friend and classmate, Samantha St. John's, Russian heritage and double-agent parents.

She typed a short e-mail to Alex, outlining her thoughts and letting her know she'd start looking into the Arachne possibility and then pushed away from her desk. She was anxious to get her broadcast over so she could get out on the streets of Suwan and find Andrea.

Tory grinned to herself as she imagined what Ben would say if he could see her. *That Athena-grad ego is going to be your downfall.* He liked to tease her but he knew that she could back up her ego with skills and action.

She'd seen another photo of him, this time supposedly in Paris at a designer party. He'd been seen with two wafer-thin supermodels and the wife of the prime minister. She'd pushed the image from her head, suppressed the impulse to ask where and how all these pictures were taken. Any conversation they might have about their relationship would focus on…the baby.

She fought the urge to put hand over her stomach. So far she'd felt nothing but the nausea. No outward signs that there was a tiny life growing inside her.

"Ready, Patton?"

She nodded, grabbed her backpack and followed Dash and Jay out of the newsroom. When they reached the market place, Tory stared into the camera, getting ready to begin her broadcast.

She glanced around her before they started, felt the determination of the people of Suwan, who'd been fighting for freedom for so long that they were worn down, but they still refused to quit. She felt for Andrea, knew her friend would have that same spirit. Andrea wouldn't let the fact that she'd been captured stop her from fighting to get free and tell these people's stories.

Dash's voice came through her earpiece as the

camera started rolling. "Tory, you're on now. Yasmine is going to talk to you directly, be ready for that."

"Good day, Tory. Bring us up to date on the situation with Andrea Jancey and her crew."

In Manhattan it was early afternoon, but in Berzhaan it was early evening. "Yasmine, a new tape of the hostages has been released to the media."

"We're running the images now," Dash said in her ear.

"As you can see, they're all unconscious and are being held together. The people or group holding them still have not revealed their name, but the demands they made with the release of the first tape were repeated. They want a total pullout of U.S. and alliance troops in less than three weeks, or they will kill all three hostages."

"Keep us up-to-date on the story."

"I will, Yasmine. Tomorrow we'll have an interview with the president of Berzhaan."

"You're clear, Tory," Dash said through her earpiece.

She waited another second until Jay turned off the camera and then walked over to the men. They started packing in their gear to head back to UBC's temporary headquarters. Tory had brought a second car because she planned to do some investigating on her own. The new video had convinced her that

Andrea's time was running out—and Tory couldn't sit in her hotel room and investigate on the computer any longer.

Tory changed into black clothing in the backseat of her car. Twilight was fading into night, and she had a small list of places she wanted to check out. Alaleh had revealed a few interesting facts when Tory had spoken to her. One was that Andrea had asked her where Kemeni rebels might be operating from if they were still in the city. Alaleh hadn't known the exact location, but word on the street had been an older section of Suwan, near Sovetski.

The second thing she'd mentioned had been that she'd noticed four men hanging around the area earlier that day dressed in djellabas and kaffiyeh, who had been speaking Berzhaani with a unique accent. She thought they were foreigners, but had no idea where they'd come from. Tory wasn't sure if that meant anything significant to her investigation but she kept it in mind.

She moved in the shadows as she watched the activity on the street, slowly winding her way from the marketplace toward Sovetski. The street was now labeled with a Berzhaani name, one more way that the country was trying to distance itself from its former Russian ties.

The smells on the street were strong and pungent. Her sense of smell had never been so keen, and she wished that it wasn't now. She felt a burning at the back of her throat and swallowed to avoid getting sick. Bile rose again, and she dashed into an alleyway to throw up. Tears came to her eyes, and she steadied herself with a few deep breaths. But she still felt a little queasy.

She leaned against the wall, trying to recover her equilibrium. She rubbed her face with the bottom of her T-shirt and waited for the weakness that had spread through her body to pass.

She never got sick. *Never.* She had to get the better of this pregnancy before it threw her completely offtrack. She refused to let it. The same way she'd always refused to let anything stop her from achieving her goals. She'd find Andrea, and then she'd deal with her condition.

She consulted the GPS unit in her phone and matched the coordinates that she'd plugged in earlier. Tory had downloaded the coordinates from their tracking software and knew that Andrea had visited this area the day she'd disappeared.

She pushed away from the wall and tucked her unit into her back pocket. Leaving the alleyway, she moved toward the newspaper stand at the end of the street. This section of Suwan was less than desirable. The tenement-type apartment housing units were worn from years of poverty and neglect. She hoped that no one stole the tires off the company car she'd left parked nearby.

Continuing down the street, she stopped at a corner newspaper stand that was built into the side of the building. She double-checked her GPS unit. Andrea had stopped there for almost ten minutes. Had it been a courier route pickup, or a contact on the Marine story?

The newsstand was closed at this hour and Tory poked under the canvas flap. The stand was secured with a simple padlock. She glanced around to make sure no one was looking, then got out her lockpicking tools and picked it. She unzipped the canvas and slipped inside. There was a small amount of space between the overhang and the magazine and newspaper racks. She sorted through the papers, searching for some clue, anything that may have been accidentally dropped—or intentionally left behind.

She pulled a penlight out of her purse and bent to search the floor. Under the cash register area, she found a note written in Berzhaani that looked like a grocery list, a couple of gum wrappers and something shiny. She put the flashlight in her mouth and reached for it. An earring. Andrea's earring! Tory had the same pair, they'd bought them together in

Phoenix to celebrate Tory's graduation from the Academy. She picked up the earring and edged backward, then stood up.

She slipped out of the canvas and rezipped it with shaking hands. The summer air was hot but not humid. Arid and dry, it sucked the moisture from her skin, and a chill shivered through her.

"Shoplifting is a crime in Berzhaan," a familiar deep voice said in Russian behind her.

"I haven't taken a thing," she replied in the same language and turned to face her lover.

Super sexy. Dangerous—though never to her. Ben looked tired and tense, but so good to her that for a minute she forgot everything—the sketchy neighborhood, the anger she'd been trying to nurse toward him and the fact that her family thought he wasn't good enough for her.

She tipped her head to the side, not really sure what to say to him now that they were face-to-face. On the phone it had been easy to let anger direct her speech, but now she wanted…hell, she didn't know what she wanted.

"I thought I told you to stay safe," he said, reaching out to capture a strand of her dark hair and tuck it behind her ear.

"I am safe. Why didn't you tell me you were in Suwan?" she asked, fighting the urge to lean against his hand. It felt like ages since they'd touched. Since she'd held him in her arms.

He took her wrist and led her up the street into an alley. He took her in his arms as soon as they were in the shadows, his mouth coming down hard on hers. She kissed him back just as fiercely.

His hands roamed down her back, creating warmth and shivers all at once as he pulled her more fully into his embrace. She pushed her hands through his hair, holding onto him as he dominated her with his kiss. As if he was staking his claim.

"Why didn't you say anything when I asked you about Andrea?" she asked as she pulled away from him. She didn't want to think about this moment— his arms around her, what it meant or didn't mean.

"I'm not at liberty to talk about my job."

She pushed out of his arms and away from him, making sure to stay in the shadows. This was the dance in which they'd been carefully engaged for the last six months. Ben, pensive and brooding, not letting a single bit of reality from his job cross into their personal lives. "Ben, you can trust me."

"This isn't about trust, Tory. You know that," he said. She wished she could still see his face.

"I'm not sure what I know about you anymore. I'm concentrating on finding Andrea right now."

"Leave that to the authorities. You're a reporter, not a cop."

"I'm just asking questions, not planning to apprehend any suspects. Speaking of which…"

"I'm not going to answer any questions."

"You were here for the Marines, right?"

"Yes."

"I saw that you got them out. Are you leaving Berzhaan soon?"

"I'm not at liberty to say. Where'd you leave your car?"

"Up the street. Why?"

"Because it's time for you to head back to your hotel."

"I'm not done yet, Ben. I have Andrea's GPS readings from her phone, and I'm retracing her steps. Her last location is close."

"Jesus, Tory. You're going to make me old before my time."

"How? This is my job."

"What if they nab you, too? What if they see you parading around the streets—"

She put her hand over his mouth. She knew that his concern stemmed from caring and all his macho stoicism was just for show. "They won't."

"Not while I'm around."

Chapter 5

Ben pulled Tory tighter in his arms. He had a job to do, but when he'd seen her, he'd had to follow. She didn't stand out. In fact, if he hadn't been so familiar with her and the way she moved, he'd never have noticed her.

She pushed against his chest, but he held her a moment longer. She seemed different, and he couldn't put his finger on what had changed. He knew that the situation wasn't ideal and figured that counted for part of it, but something…

"What are you doing here?" she asked.

He saw no reason to keep the truth from her. "One

of my men was kidnapped with Andrea. We're going after him. After all of them," he said.

"The translator," she breathed. "Of course. I can help you." She pulled out a small notebook and glanced at it. "I've been doing a lot of research. I'm getting close to figuring out what happened when they were taken."

He framed her face with his hands, stared down into her eyes and felt something shift inside him. "I know you can help, babe, but I want you safe. The streets of Suwan are dangerous at night. Too many leaderless rebels still want to fight for a cause they don't believe is dead."

"Why is that? Why do men keep killing even when a cause is lost?"

He couldn't tell her what he knew. That men fought because it was what they were bred to do. That once a man went to war, became a warrior, it was hard to go back to living a life without battles.

He feared that he was much like these leaderless Kemeni, and that he'd spend his life after LASER searching for something to replace the primitive rush that being a warrior gave him.

"I don't know," he said at last. "You need to go back to your hotel."

"I will. But I found Andrea's earring at that news-stand. I think I'm on the right track."

"May I see it?" he asked. They'd found nothing at Paul's last coordinates to prove the man had been there.

She held up a small turquoise stone set in silver. "But you don't know when she was here, do you?"

Tory looked at her notes. "Four days ago, in the afternoon. We tracked her down this street. I've got one final location to check, the place she was before the signal disappeared."

Ben scratched his chin, at war with himself. He wanted her out of the night, back in her hotel room, but he also wanted her keen eyes and investigative skills. "What are the coordinates?"

Tory rattled them off and he frowned again. Naturally they were the same as Manning's last known location. His men were nearby, looking for something that would point them toward Paul. Tory was already a step ahead of them.

He wanted Tory away from the area. But this was her job. She was an investigative reporter. She needed to investigate, to solve puzzles the same way he needed to protect, serve, be a warrior.

"Why didn't you just tell me you were looking for Andrea?" she asked.

"I wasn't at that time."

"But now you are?"

"Yes," he said.

"Because of your man?"

"Partly."

"Can I get an answer from you that's more than one word?"

"Maybe."

She tipped her head to the side and gave him one of her long, measuring looks. "You try a woman's patience, Bennington."

He bit back a grin. "Do tell."

"Not now. I'm working."

"Later, then. Tell me what you've got so far."

"You first."

"You already know what I know," he said.

"I'm still not sure why you didn't tell me you were here."

"I couldn't. You know I can't ever talk about it."

She nodded. "How did you spot me?"

"Your walk."

"What about it?"

"It's distinctly you, Athena grad. Part seductive hip-swaying, part arrogant swagger, total ballsy attitude that says don't mess with me."

"Then why *are* you messing with me?" she asked, with that sassy attitude that made him want to kiss her or spank her.

"Because I can handle you," he said, though a part of him wondered if he really could. He'd asked her to stay away but she'd put her job before him and come anyway. Still, he wasn't saying he didn't understand her actions....

"You think so?"

"I know so. Do you want to see the last sight before you go back to your hotel?"

She took two steps away from him and gave him her on-air smile. It was all teeth and just this side of sweet. "Newsflash, Forsythe, I was already planning to."

He fought against the urge to smile back. "Newsflash? Is that an industry term?"

"Yes, it is. Like those acronyms you use all the time."

"What, like ASAP?"

She gave him the finger and kept walking. She stayed to the shadows and moved with cool efficiency. Ben covered her but knew he didn't have to protect her. Tory was more than able to hold her own.

That didn't make him feel better about having her out here. He took her arm and pulled her behind him as they reached the corner. The GPS coordinates were for a park in the middle of the high-rise apartment buildings.

"Let me go first," he said.

"Why?"

"Because we've already seen a few drug dealers in the park. I think we scared them off...."

"I can handle drug dealers, Ben. I did a story on the park behind the New York library that used to be a haven for them some years ago."

He turned, pinning her to the wall. He held her hips loosely in his grip.

"Ben, I've missed you, too, but now is not the time."

"Someone's coming," he said under his breath.

She nodded against his chest, and then wrapped her arms around him. His body reacted immediately to the threat and the woman in his arms.

He bent his head to her neck, tasting the smooth skin revealed there. "Can you see them?"

She shifted around in his arms. "Yes. They've stopped two houses down."

"Are they armed?" he asked.

She moved subtly to the left. "Yes. Some kind of assault riffle. Two men both a little shorter than you. They are moving again."

He shifted slightly to confirm they weren't his team. Dammit, no.

"Slip your hand under my shirt. I have a sidearm in a holster at the small of my back," he ordered.

Tory slipped her hands under his shirt past the warm skin and felt the cold hard steel of Ben's weapon. The familiar feel of adrenaline rushing through her body brought with it the heady cocktail that was nerves and excitement.

Her fingers felt sweaty and she forced herself to breathe deeply. The scent of Ben's cologne filled her nostrils and helped her find her inner balance. Still, she didn't make a move to grab the gun, just held her fingers over the weapon, ready to draw it if they were threatened.

She had experience with firearms but truthfully she was a reporter, not some sort of mercenary. Her microphone was her best weapon. She knew she could handle herself in unarmed combat but hoped it wouldn't come to that. She thought about the baby and knew she didn't want to endanger her child in any way.

She didn't know if she could kill anyone, either. Not again. The face of the last—and only—man, thank God, she'd killed had stayed with her. It had been on Puerto Isla, when she'd met Ben. She would wake up in the middle of the night, seeing those eyes, and the man's shock when her knife had entered his body. She'd had no choice—it had been kill or be killed—but that didn't change the fact that she had blood on her hands.

This the first time since Puerto Isla that she'd been in this kind of situation. For a moment a grim sense of humor flashed through her. Only with Ben did she get into situations where she had to defend her life.

What kind of life did he lead? What kind of life would their child have, with both parents involved in dangerous professions?

"Okay?"

She realized she was trembling a little. "Yes. I won't let you down."

"I know that, babe."

"When are you going to lay off calling me *babe?*" she asked, teasing him, trying to relieve the tension in her own body as the armed men moved closer to their location.

"Never," he said, brushing his lips against hers. It was reassuring in the way nothing else could have been, to have him so close to her. Ben might call her "babe" and tease her mercilessly but he also trusted her in tight situations.

His forehead pressed to hers. "My men are out there. They'll cover us."

"Do you think these two are a threat?" Tory asked. There had been outbreaks of violence and fighting all over the city since the attempted coup back in February. A coup an Athena grad subverted. She smiled, remembering being on the spot to inter-view Selena Shaw Jones as she emerged, battered but triumphant, from the capitol building.

"I hope not." She heard in his voice not real hope or even fear. Just acceptance of what he'd been called to do. She wanted to cradle him closer to her, this man of hers, this warrior who'd been fighting nonstop since…well, for as long as she'd known him.

"Do you think they saw Andrea?" Tory asked, because to her mind that was their only objective. Find Andrea and get her safely back to the United States.

"Unknown."

She heard the soft voice through his earpiece.

"Three in position behind you," a man said.

"Four in range to take out target," a second voice added.

"Hold," Ben said.

Ben looked at her. "What are the two men doing?"

Tory shifted her head for a better glimpse of the gunmen and saw them disappear up the steps of an apartment building. "They entered that building, the one with the streetlamp out in front of it. I think we should go and question them. If they patrol these streets, they're potential witnesses."

The building was right across the street from Andrea's last known location. Someone in that building could have seen what happened that day, or at least heard something that could point them in the right direction.

"No," he said carefully.

"I wasn't asking," she said. She understood the need for caution but if those men lived on this street, she wanted to talk to them.

"Four, can you still see them?"

"Adjusting scope. Yes, sir, I can see them."

"How many men are with you?" Tory asked.

"Five," Ben said impatiently.

"I can't see them."

"That's because they're the best."

"I'm glad. Did you train them?"

"I trained with them."

"I've got them," Four said.

Tory had no desire to be the main feature on the news tonight, part of an outbreak of violence in a city that desperately needed peace and rebuilding. This section of Suwan had some resemblance to the gang-controlled inner cities of America. Violence could break out at any time. "You aren't going to shoot those men, are you?"

Ben looked down at her. "If I have to."

"Let me go in and talk to them."

"Never. This is not the nicest section of town, Patton."

"Families live here, Ben. Moms, kids…they've seen enough violence."

He didn't say anything else, just pushed away

from her. There was no need for them to pretend to be making out. There was no one to hide from.

"Come into the building with me. I want to ask some questions. Maybe someone in there saw Andrea the day she was kidnapped."

"Dammit, Patton."

She forced herself not to smile at the frustration in his voice. "I'll take the lead on this one."

"Four, what's the activity?"

"Seems like a sentry on guard duty."

"Sentry?"

"Yes, sir."

"What's your plan, Patton?"

"Knock on the doors and ask to talk to the women. Andrea was interviewing female activists who are pushing for the right to vote. Her notes indicate that she spoke to one, a young mother, at the corner newsstand."

"Nothing like stirring the pot."

"What's your idea?"

"We enter the building and ask questions of anyone we encounter at gunpoint."

"Is that the only way?"

"It's the easiest way."

"For Rambo, maybe. What if an innocent gets shot?"

He didn't say anything to her.

"Can't you protect me if I walk in there?"

"Yes. But it will end with violence if something happens."

"Since that's your plan anyway…."

He cursed under his breath and turned away from her for a minute. "If we do this, you follow my lead."

"I think I should ask the questions. People really do like to talk to me."

He cupped her face in his hands. And leaned down to kiss her. It was a sweet kiss and totally unexpected. "I'm proud of the way you do your job. Let me do mine."

"Okay."

"I'm going in with the reporter. She's going to ask some questions.

"Cover us."

Ben stayed at her side as they entered the lobby area of the apartment building. The two men they'd seen on the streets immediately came to their feet, guns resting loosely in their hands. Ben's hand went to the small of his back.

She stepped in front of him, out of shooting range if he had to use his weapon, smiling at the men.

"I'm Tory Patton with UBC News," she said in Russian, taking her press badge from her pocket and showing the men.

She repeated her name and affiliation in Berzhaani. The man closest to her lowered the muzzle of his weapon.

He was tall, almost Ben's height, and had hazel green eyes and a close-cropped beard. He wore desert camouflage clothing and a covering on his head.

The other man had brown eyes and no beard, and watched her with suspicion.

"What do you want?" the tall man asked in Berzhaani.

"To speak to you."

Tory glanced at Ben. "How good is your Berzhaani?"

"Better than yours. You just told him you wanted to mouth at him."

"Will you translate?"

"Sure." Ben moved to her side, both hands in the open, and spoke to the two men.

The three of them shared a laugh, probably about her command of Berzhaani, and she noted that they relaxed their grip on their weapons.

"Ask them if they saw Andrea." Tory took a picture of her friend from her purse.

She noticed that one of the men lifted the muzzle of his gun as she did it.

Ben quickly said something to the man but he

didn't relax until she had the photo in her hand and passed it to him. Both men studied the picture.

"We haven't seen her," the first man said in English.

Tory raised an eyebrow. The men had understood everything she and Ben had said.

"I'd like to interview the people in this building about the recent changes in Suwan," she said, picking up English herself.

"I doubt that anyone will want to talk to you."

She glanced at Ben and he shrugged. He'd stay if she found a way to get these two men to talk.

"What's your name?" she asked the tall man.

"Foroohar. And this is Kambiz."

"I'm Tory and this is Ben," she said. "How long have you both lived here?"

"We grew up here," Foroohar said.

"In this neighborhood?" Tory asked again, wanting a clear picture of the two men.

"Yes."

"Are you related?" Tory wasn't sure how to proceed. Instinct told her the men had to know someone who saw something on the day Andrea and her crew were taken. But how to get them to talk?

"Just friends. Why are you asking all these questions?"

"Because my friend has been taken hostage and

my government can't meet the demands of the men who have her. And I…I want to do what I can to find her and bring her home safely."

The men exchanged a look and then nodded to each other. Kambiz stepped forward and held out his hand. "Come with me."

"Why?"

"I have someone you can talk to. But not out here."

Ben stepped forward. "I'm going with her."

"Is she yours?" Kambiz asked.

Ben nodded. Just like that, Tory was put into the role of a second-class citizen. She was pushed to the side while these two men made the decisions. She knew that these men were used to thinking of women in different terms, but her all-American feminist side wanted to smack Ben for agreeing with the men.

"She will be safe."

"All the same, I'm coming along."

"You'll have to leave your weapon here."

Ben pulled his gun and unloaded the cartridge, tossing it to Foroohar. "You hold that for me."

Ben walked in front of her down the hallway to the stairs. Tory felt a moment's fear for Ben. He was unarmed but not entirely weaponless, and she knew he'd give his life to protect her.

Kambiz led them up three flights of stairs to

number 1645 and glanced back at them. She saw in his eyes something she couldn't define, yet at the same time it was a look she'd seen in Ben's eyes, and in the eyes of her brother and father. A man coming home.

He opened the door. "Golshan?"

A feminine voice replied in Berzhaani, too quickly for Tory to follow.

Ben leaned closer to her, translating the conversation quietly under his breath. "She's in the bedroom with the kids.

"There is an American reporter here," Kambiz said. "She wants to ask some questions about the American hostages."

"Well, bring her in."

Kambiz stepped over the threshold and gestured for them to follow. The living room of the apartment was small, but nicely decorated. An overstuffed couch dominated the room with a coffee table littered with books and papers in front of it. A large table sat against one wall, the remains of a meal still on it.

A very pretty woman with dark skin and black hair came into the room. She had pulled her hair back in a chignon and her blue eyes were lined with kohl, making them stand out.

"My wife, Golshon," Kambiz said.

"I'm Tory Patton. I speak horrible Berzhaani," she said to the woman.

Golshan nodded. "I speak some English."

"This is Ben. He can translate for us."

"Let's try your language first. My father was a diplomat and I had the opportunity to learn English," Golshan said.

An older woman came out of the kitchen and started clearing the table.

"My mother," Golshan said. "Would you like some tea?"

"Thank you."

She spoke to her mother in Berzhaani and gestured for Tory and Ben to have a seat on the couch. Ben declined, leaning against the wall. Kambiz stayed standing as well. But Tory took a seat and Golshan gave her a look that said—men!

"Have you heard about the American news team that was taken hostage?"

"Yes, I have."

"I believe that they were in your neighborhood the day they were taken. Did you see anything?"

Golshan glanced at her husband and then her mother. They watched her carefully, leaving the decision of what she would say up to Golshan. Tory handed Golshan Andrea's picture.

"This woman is like a sister to me. A little sister

who looked up to me and followed me into this pro-
fession. I need to find her. If you can help me in any
way, I'd appreciate it."

Golshan looked down at the picture. "Yes, I saw
her on that day."

"Did you see anything else?"

Golshan nodded and leaned closer to Tory. "I saw
them take her."

Chapter 6

Ben watched Tory talk to Golshan, and was impressed by the way she carefully asked questions and led the other woman to where Tory wanted to go. He also listened to his men, who were keeping him posted on the activity on the street. There were other armed men out there. The neighborhood seemed a dichotomy to him.

This apartment was cozy, homey, clearly a place that was filled with a family who cared for one another. Yet the streets were patrolled by men with guns who wouldn't hesitate to use them.

"May I record our interview?" Tory asked, taking out a mini-recorder.

Golshan looked at her husband and Ben noticed that Kambiz nodded slightly.

"Yes."

Tory set up the recorder, handing her a small microphone. "Clip this to your shirt."

Golshan attached the microphone and Tory took a notebook from that huge bag of hers. She smiled at the other woman and Ben felt a swelling of pride as he watched Tory go to work.

"What happened, Golshan? Take me through what you saw."

"Your friend…she was speaking into the camera. Not talking to anyone else, just her."

"She wasn't interviewing anyone?" Tory asked.

"No."

Ben's men had been following a cold trail. There was nothing left in the spot where Andrea had been taping. He knew she hadn't been shooting live—otherwise the world would have seen the abduction. He wondered where the tape had gone.

"Did she speak to anyone before going on camera?" Tory asked.

"I don't think so. I didn't see her speak to anyone."

"What happened next?" Tory asked. Ben continued to admire the way she led Golshan through the events without interfering with her telling of the story. It was one of the things that made Tory stand out as a reporter. She made whomever she was interviewing feel as if they were chatting with a friend.

"Two cars pulled in around them. Armed men jumped out of each vehicle. They fired shots, overpowered your friend and the two men with her. They tossed them and their equipment in the trunks of the cars and drove off."

"Where were you when it happened?"

"Downstairs, with my children, Nikoo and Peyam. We had the door open and were about to step into the street. Nikoo was lagging behind and Peyam had just stepped outside."

"What did you do?"

"I grabbed the back of his shirt and pulled him back inside."

"Was anyone else hurt?"

"One of our neighbors. He was hit in the leg."

Even across the room Ben saw the lingering fear in Golshan's eyes. She glanced to the hallway that he assumed led to her sleeping children, one hand going to her throat.

Tory placed her hand on Golshan's arm. "How old are your children?"

"They are eight. Twins, but very different."

"Were they scared?" Tory asked. "Were you? I can't imagine what I'd feel at such a moment."

"I didn't think of anything except pulling them inside the building, shielding them with my body. My son, Peyam, wanted to watch, but I held him to me."

Kambiz went to his wife and put his hand on her shoulder. She covered his hand with her own, glancing up at her husband. And Ben felt like an intruder in the moment. Tory paused before asking her next question.

"How long did the incident take?" Tory asked.

Golshan dropped her hand, but her fingers still trembled. Kambiz stayed close to his wife. Ben saw in the man something of himself. These two represented what he felt for Tory. He saw at once that Kambiz wished he'd been at home that day when his family came so close to harm.

"I don't know. Maybe five minutes."

"Had Andrea been in this area before?" Tory asked, sounding calm. Ben wondered how she did it. How she turned off her emotions and kept to her line of questioning. Because he knew her well enough to know that she'd be empathetic to Golshan.

Golshan shook her head. "I hadn't noticed her prior to that day. This is a quiet neighborhood. Our men patrol the streets. We haven't seen as much unrest as certain other areas of the city."

"Can you describe the men involved?"

"Not really. They wore Kaffiyeh and light colored robes. I didn't recognize any of them."

"So they weren't from your neighborhood?" Tory asked.

"I don't think so. But to be honest it happened so quickly and I was concerned for my children."

Tory glanced over at Kambiz. "I notice your husband is armed."

Kombiz reached for his wife's hand and she took it. Ben saw determination in their eyes. "My mother and sister live with us, as do our children. Protecting our family is Kambiz's duty. Since the hostages were taken, many men here have armed themselves."

Tory nodded. Ben suspected she liked this family. He knew he did. "You have all banded together to protect your community."

"Yes. I have some training. All of the men in our building and two across the street are keeping watch."

"Have there been any other incidents since they started patrolling?"

"No."

Tory finished up her interview just as Ben's earpiece buzzed.

"Leader, this is Three. We've got some movement two streets over."

"Take Two and investigate."

"Yes, sir."

Tory glanced over at him. "I think it's time we left," he said.

"If you see anything else or remember any details, will you give me a call? I'm staying at the Sheraton Suwan." Tory wrote her name on a slip of paper and handed it to Golshan, who nodded.

"Thank you. You gave us more information than we had before."

"I hope you find your friend," Golshan said.

"I'm sure we will," Tory said before gathering her stuff. Together, she and Ben left the apartment and headed out into the night.

Ben led the way out of the building. She knew he'd be heading off to join his men, and she worried about him. "I guess this is where we part ways."

The night air was cooler than it had been earlier. It stirred her hair around her face. Ben looked down at her with that fierce gaze of his that she couldn't always read. "You are one hell of a woman."

"I know. Athena Academy breeds us for excellence."

"It's more than Athena training. It's something that comes from inside you."

She wondered if he saw that fabled pregnancy glow and hoped not. She wanted to tell him when they were both safely away from danger and able to really talk.

"Well, maybe it's just because you haven't seen me in a while."

She hadn't seen this side of herself for a while, either. Tonight was further confirmation that she liked being in the field a lot more than being behind the anchor desk. The chance to interview real people. To be with Golshan in the moment and feel her emotions as she recounted what she'd seen…nothing Tory did in Manhattan compared with that.

"No, there's something more."

"I've been thinking that being an anchor isn't what I really want to do. Ty said this is my last field assignment."

"What else would you do? Leave UBC?"

"I have no idea. I don't want to get out of the business…this really isn't the time for this discussion."

He stroked his hand down the side of her face. "No, it isn't. When you were talking to Golshan, I realized that your job was more than a career to you. It was humbling because I'd been thinking…"

"That I should have stayed in Manhattan."

He flushed a little. "Babe, I can't change overnight."

"It's been a year."

"I've had thirty-five to get the way I am. Give me time."

But time was running out for them. For the relationship they were both still trying to figure out. And seeing what had happened with Andrea made her realize how random life could be. Realize that, no matter what Tory's plans and goals were, life could be interrupted at any moment.

"I've got to catch up with my men. Thanks for suggesting we go talk to them. Threatening Kambiz would have been a mistake."

"Do you make those kinds of mistakes often?"

"I hope not, but because we're usually on the move, we don't have time to acknowledge they are mistakes."

"Your world scares me, Forsythe."

"Some days it does me, too."

"Why do you do it?" she asked. She really wanted to know. Had wanted to know for a long time now, but never had the guts to actually ask him.

"I can't *not* do it. I can't explain it properly."

"Try," she said.

"Are you interviewing me, Patton?"

"Maybe. Make me understand."

"My life—my cover life—socializing, jet-setting, is so superficial that I need something that makes me remember I'm alive."

"What about me?" she asked. The words slipped out before she could stop them.

"You make me feel vibrantly alive, but you're very independent. I don't think you'd take to a man who spent his days waiting for you."

He was right. She knew he was right.

"I'm going back to the hotel. UBC is using a small ballroom as a remote broadcast center."

"Let me walk you back to your car."

She didn't need that and wanted some time by herself to regain her equilibrium. What if she threw up again? It wasn't the way she wanted Ben to find out he was going to be a father.

"I'll be fine. Go join your men and see what you can find out. I'm going to do some research, see if I can find out what happened to the tape that Andrea was shooting when she was kidnapped."

Ben nodded. He kissed her, hard. "I'll try to come to your hotel room tonight."

"I'm in 3022," she said, starting to move away from him.

He cocked his head to the side. "If I don't make it…"

She tried to smile but couldn't, because the words that were sometimes a joke between them now took on serious significance. This enemy wasn't someone Ben could evade, but rather a man he'd have to confront. "I'll assume the best, that I'll hear from you when you can call."

He tugged her back into his arms, smiling down at her. "Assume that I'm missing you."

"You, too."

She pivoted and walked away before she did something totally ridiculous and begged him to stay with her. Begged him not to go do the job he'd been trained to do. Begged him to stay safe, because she was coming to realize that she didn't want to live without him.

A burst of gunfire exploded behind her, and she ducked out of the line of fire. Ben was already there, grabbing her arm and dragging her behind him, off the sidewalk and into the shadows.

"Dammit. Do you have a weapon?" he demanded.

"My knife is in my bag."

"Get it out." He pulled his gun and stood in front of her.

She reached in her bag and took out the hunting knife her dad had given her when she was eight.

"Where are your men?"

"Coming in behind these shooters."

A sound at the other end of the side street had her turning. She slipped away from Ben farther into the shadows to give him a clear shot at the two assailants. They let out a burst of semiautomatic fire and dove for cover.

Ben returned their fire, but it was impossible to tell if they'd been hit. There was an eerie stillness in the darkened alley, and Tory's ears were filled with the rapid beating of her heart. And her own breaths as she tried to keep them silent.

Ben moved to her left. "Let's move toward them." His words were practically silent.

"I'll take the right," she whispered.

He nodded. She watched him blend seamlessly into the shadows and move toward the left. Then he was gone. She left her bag beside the Dumpster, closed her eyes and focused her senses. Listening for things that were out of place. She heard it then, the rustle of cloth against the building.

Moving lightly on her feet, she edged closer to the sound. She held her knife loosely in her right hand, tucked against her black clothing so the blade didn't glint.

As her eyes adjusted to the darkness, she made out the silhouette of a man crouched low to the ground, assault rifle held competently in his arms as he scanned the alley, waiting for her or Ben to make a mistake.

Tory halted her forward progress and waited until he scanned the area away from her. Quickly she ran forward and attacked his back. Holding the knife to his throat she growled, "Drop your weapon."

Ben's focus blurred for a second as Tory moved into position behind the gunman and held her knife to his throat. He heard footsteps behind him and knew they were surrounded.

First he dealt with the threat to Tory. She was too close to survive if the gunman fired. The guy lifted his weapon and Ben knew Tory would be dead in a second. He lifted his Sig-Sauer and fired. One bullet right between the assailant's eyes. Tory stood frozen, blood spattering on her.

The other man lifted his gun. Ben pivoted and brought his weapon up sighted on the man. They stood like that for a few seconds, maybe three.

"Drop it or die," Ben said in Berzhaani.

"If he doesn't get you, I will," Kambiz said behind him.

Ben couldn't negotiate or play games while Tory was in the alley with him. The man dropped his gun and fell to his knees at Ben's feet. Ben cuffed him with the zipcord he always carried and picked up the gun.

"Thanks," Ben said to Kambiz. He was surprised the other man had come into the alleyway.

"You're welcome."

"Do you know this man?"

Kambiz moved closer to the man, to inspect him. "He's not part of my patrol. Maybe Kemeni militia?"

"My men are coming. Kambiz, will you go get Golshan and ask her to come and look at these men? To see if she recognized them from the abduction?"

Kambiz stared at him for a minute, man to man, each of them aware that they had a woman to protect. "I'll ask her."

Kambiz left and Tory walked over to him. She looked pale. "Dammit, are you okay?"

"I'm fine."

He pulled her into his arms, she trembled against him. "I'm sorry, babe. I should have injured him or warned you but there was no time. I had to—"

She put her fingers over his lips. "Thank you for saving my life."

"I know you can do the job yourself, only there wasn't time."

"Ben, seriously, I appreciate what you did. I know I like to take care of myself but I think I would have died if you hadn't been here. I would have taken him with me…."

He gripped her shoulders, wanting to shake her hard and yell at her to get her ass back to New York where she'd be safe. But as he stared down into her face, saw the fine trembling of her lips, he knew she realized the danger they were both in. God, how had he come to this?

He hugged her to him with one arm, keeping his gun trained on the handcuffed man with the other.

"This is leader, where the hell are you guys?" Ben asked into his wireless mic.

"Coming in behind you. We've got two prisoners," Salvo said.

"I've got one," Ben said.

"You let one get away? Slick's losing his touch." Salvo, Velosi and Georgie entered the side street.

"Funny, Salvo. He didn't get away. He's dead."

Tory stepped away from him and stood on her own. Now that someone else could witness her weakness, it was gone. His heart softened toward her when he realized that the tough-girl act was still in place as far as the world could observe. He was the only one who saw the vulnerable woman.

Ben's team converged on them from the darkness. The only one Tory would know from Puerto Isla was Robert O'Neill, and he could already see her smiling at the tech man.

"Hey," she said. "Long time no see."

"Still asking your questions?" O'Neill asked.

"Yep. Got to keep you boys on your toes."

Ben needed to get Tory out of there. The less she saw of his team, the better. Having too much info could put her in more danger.

He turned to the medic, moving between him and Tory to keep her from getting a good look. "Velosi, check him out. I'm pretty sure it was a clean hit."

Velosi knelt beside the gunman and felt for a pulse.

"He's gone?"

"Affirmative. We'll take him back to base with us and I'll document this. Do you want to keep Ms. Patton out of this report?"

Ben glanced at Tory and she shrugged. "If you need my statement…"

"I'll get Ms. Patton's statement later."

"Yes, sir. Georgie, can you give me a hand with the body?"

"Sure thing."

Velosi and Georgie lifted the dead body and carried it to the end of the alley where their vehicle was parked. They gathered the prisoners and settled them in the back of the vehicle. Ben stayed a little behind with Tory.

"There's no way we're all going to fit in there," Salvo said.

"I can give you guys a ride," Tory called.

Ben wanted nothing more than to send his men back to the base and take Tory someplace and just hold her. To reassure himself that she was safe and unharmed. To have her in his arms for one night and keep the nightmare of this evening's events at bay.

Ben glanced at her. "Thanks, but we'll find our own way back."

"Won't that be hard?"

"No, Patton. It won't be."

"I think you're being stubborn."

He couldn't believe she was arguing with him in front of his men. "We're supposed to be low profile. We can't travel with a reporter."

"Fine," she said, anger underlying every word she spoke. "Good night then. It's been real."

She stalked out of the alley. Ben watched her leave, realizing that there would always be something unsettled between them because of his job. He wished he'd managed to keep her out of danger. But instead he'd dragged her into the center of it.

"Salvo, make sure she gets to her car safely."

"Yes, sir," Lewis said, moving quickly and silently to follow Tory.

"We have a witness to the abduction. Get all the men together in that lamp light to make IDing the captured men easier."

"Good idea, boss."

Kambiz showed up a few minutes later with Golshan. She was veiled and not even her eyes were discernible. She held Kambiz's hand as she moved closer to the prisoners. She moved carefully past each bound man, hesitating next to the dead body and murmuring a prayer over him before coming back to her husband's side.

"Well?"

"Those aren't the men I saw," Golshan said carefully, in Berzhaani.

"Are you sure?" Ben asked, questioning to make sure she didn't have any doubts.

"Yes, I am."

Ben nodded. "Thank you. Both of you. I'm sorry to have asked you to come out here for such a gruesome task."

"You are very welcome. I will be available to help you in any way. Kambiz, let's go home."

The couple walked away and Ben turned to his men. O'Neill, Georgie and Potchicki rode in the military vehicle with the prisoners. Salvo liberated a late model sedan for himself, Ben and Velosi to use. They'd leave it somewhere to be found later.

The ride back to the base was quick but the paperwork and debriefings were long. Ben's blood chilled when their prisoners grudgingly admitted to spotting Tory and Ben entering the apartment and planning to capture them to use as leverage against the Berzhaan government. The men had connections to the Kemeni and wanted to free the rebels who had been imprisoned after the capitol building takeover last February.

It was well after midnight when Ben left. It was time to attend to his unfinished business with Tory— and convince her to go home.

Chapter 7

Tory walked through the lobby of the hotel, hoping to avoid meeting anyone. She had blood spattered on her pants, she'd gotten sick in the car and she really just wanted to find a quiet place to hide.

"Patton, didn't anyone tell you that a television reporter should always look ready to step in front of the camera?"

Tory put on her on-air smile and glanced over at Shannon Conner. Of course the blonde would be immaculately groomed and look like something out of a fashion magazine, while Tory felt as if she'd been steamrolled.

"This is what a real journalist looks like, Conner. I've been doing fieldwork."

Shannon hitched her Burberry bag up higher on her shoulder and gave Tory a look that she remembered from their first meeting at Athena Academy more than fifteen years earlier. That "I'm better than you" look.

"Really? Where?" Shannon asked.

"In Suwan. The city is in an interesting state right now. What are you doing in the lobby at this time of night?" Tory asked. It seemed to her that Shannon was always lurking about. Waiting for something to happen so she could get the scoop. Normally Tory would plan to stay up, too, but tonight, she wanted only her bed and some privacy.

Wait a minute. Where did that come from? She wasn't about to be out-scooped by Shannon, or any other reporter for that matter.

Sparring with Shannon was exactly what she needed to keep her mind off of the close call she and Ben had had tonight.

"I'm glad you stopped me, Shannon. I've been wanting to talk to you about the hostage story. Do you have time for a few questions?"

Shannon gave her that barracuda smile that had won her accolades for being a tough-as-nails journalist. "What kind?"

"About kidnapped journalists and the stories you've been reporting." Fishing for information was one of her favorite parts of the job. There was the give-and-take where each reporter lured the other one with half truths. And the one with the best poker face usually won.

"I guess I could give you five minutes."

"Thanks," Tory said. Let the games begin. She glanced around for a place where they could talk undisturbed. She led the way to two chairs nestled in an alcove just off the main lobby.

"How did you get the first hostage tape? Was it delivered to you or to ABS?"

Shannon leaned back in her chair, the picture of ease and relaxation. "I got it from a source who came to me, not the studio."

"Why you?"

"I was in the right place at the right time, Tory."

"Coincidence, huh?"

"Maybe they just wanted to give it to the best."

"Or maybe they thought you were the one who was going to be abducted."

"What makes you say that?"

"The fact that there were two blond reporters in the area. A couple of people I spoke to in the marketplace both mentioned seeing a blonde. Not you or Andrea by name. Made me wonder if Andrea got nabbed because of a story you were covering. Plus, they sent the tape to your network. Andrea's new, they might not have realized she worked for UBC."

Shannon sank back in her chair and it was impossible to read anything on the other woman's face. "I didn't think about that. I've been covering the push for women's votes, and I believe Andrea was as well."

"Yes, she was. I haven't had a chance to review all of your reports from Suwan. Who have you interviewed?"

"No one woman in particular. I know Andrea was following Alaleh and her friends. I talked to different women all the time, in different socioeconomic backgrounds."

"Have you noticed anyone following you?"

"No. And I'm always watching my back."

"Why?"

"I've made enemies, Patton. Surely you can understand that."

Tory felt a bit of comradeship with Shannon for the first time in a long time. "I can understand that. There's always someone out there who's quicker and younger."

Shannon nodded. "Do you have any more questions?"

"Just one. Who gave you the first tape?"

"You know I can't reveal my source."

Tory knew Shannon was hiding something from her. "I spoke to an eyewitness of the abduction tonight. Would you be willing to give me a description of your source so I can run it past her?"

"No, but I'd be happy to talk to your eyewitness and see where it leads."

"I'm going to have to pass on that opportunity."

"Thought you would."

Tory stood. "Good night."

She walked to the elevators, processing all the information she'd gathered. Shannon wasn't giving anything away and she hoped that Joan had gotten somewhere with her contacts at ABS.

She entered her room and dropped her bag then leaned back against the door for support. She was so tired.

The message light flashed on her phone and she went to retrieve the message, flipping on the light as she walked to the desk. She plugged in her computer to the DSL port and listened to the message from Joan, telling Tory that she was meeting with Shannon's producer in the morning for coffee.

While her e-mail downloaded, she stripped out of her dirty clothes, tossing them on the chair. Catching a glimpse of herself in the mirror, she stared at her body, wanting to see some indication of the baby that was nestled inside her.

But she saw nothing, no change. She put her hand over her stomach, trying to connect to the baby, but again felt nothing. Aside from the nausea, there was no sign of a baby.

Baby, lover, career. All of these things circled through her thoughts. It was easier to focus on the puzzle of why Andrea and her crew had been taken and who had abducted them.

She hoped Ben would get some information from the men they'd captured tonight. She rubbed her temples as she remembered the instant she'd thought she was going to die. When she realized she'd seriously misjudged the man she'd attacked. She rarely misjudged people. At least, she hadn't in the past.

Could her time in the anchor chair be slowing her down? Was she losing her edge in the field? It wasn't just her brush with death that had her questioning herself. Something had changed in her mind when she'd sat down across from Shannon. She no longer saw someone who was a competitor, but someone who was in a different place in her life and her career.

Ben opened the lock on Tory's hotel room door using the manager's key card he'd swiped from the front desk. He eased into the room. There was a glow from the computer in the corner, but otherwise the room was completely dark.

He eyed the empty bed. Nothing had moved since he'd entered the room. Where was Tory? Tonight had given him a scare like he'd never experienced before. Was it possible she'd felt the same?

Well, he'd be here whenever she appeared.

Quietly he stripped out of his clothes, folding them into a neat pile and leaving them on the dresser. He took a step toward the bed, lifting the covers to ease into the bed when he felt the air stir behind him.

Tory grabbed him around the throat with her left arm, and took hold of his right wrist with her right hand. "Gotcha."

The cool cotton of her T-shirt rubbed against his back. "What are you going to do to with me?"

"Whatever I want, Slick. Isn't that what your men call you?" She caressed his neck with her fingers, rubbing his pulse point.

"Yes," he said, bringing his left hand up to grasp her left wrist, covering her moving fingers with his own. "But they're being smart-asses when they say it."

"What makes you think I'm any different?" she asked in that silky voice of hers that stroked down his spine like a caress.

He held her hand firmly in his grip and shifted his

weight, flipping her over his shoulder so that she landed face-up on the bed. He followed her down quickly, settling himself on top of her.

"Got you."

"Do you really think I didn't let you?" she asked, her arms wrapping around his shoulders as her legs shifted so that he was nestled between them.

He loved this woman. He didn't know what to do with her half the time, but he loved her feisty spirit and the way she always kept him on his toes.

He leaned down and kissed her. She bit at his lower lip, sucking it between her teeth. He groaned deep in his throat and with one hand, stroked each breast through the T-shirt. Her nipples responded immediately to his touch.

She gasped and he thrust his tongue into her mouth. He captured her wrists and held them to the bed by her head. He undulated against her, using his entire body to stroke hers.

"Link your fingers together and put them behind your neck."

"What makes you think you're in charge?" she asked, rubbing her toes up the back of his leg.

"Aren't I?" he asked, pushing his hand up under her T-shirt and feeling her smooth skin.

He put both hands on her waist and lowered his head to her chest, listening to the steady beat of her heart. He'd almost lost her tonight. He wanted to spank her for the worry she'd caused him. Escort her down to the airport, put her sexy ass on a plane and send her back to the States.

"Ben?"

She ran her hands down his back, holding him close to her. He shuddered at her touch and knew it was more than physical. "I thought I said hands behind your neck."

He felt the minute shifting of her body beneath his and was ready when she pushed her heels against the bed and rolled them over. When he was underneath her he pulled the T-shirt from her body and tossed it aside. He cupped her breasts with both hands, rubbing his thumbs over her nipples.

She shifted on top of him, straddling him. She wasn't wearing any underwear. He felt the humid wetness at the apex of her thighs and he hardened painfully. He shifted his hips, rubbing his length along the center of her body.

She moaned his name, scraping her fingernails down his chest. He slid his hands down her torso until he had her hips in his hands. He teased her with the tip of his erection, rubbing it at the gate of her body. Her hips rolled against his and he groaned at the feel of her, so hot against him.

He could feel his own readiness and knew he

wasn't going to last much longer. He thrust up into her and rolled so that she was once again underneath him.

Fully seated inside her body, he held himself still even though he wanted to thrust until he came. He angled his head and caught the tip of her left breast between his teeth. He bit carefully on it and then suckled her deep into his mouth.

She shifted beneath him, trying to move herself on his cock but he held her underneath, completely under his will. In bed was the only time he ever felt as if he had control of the wildfire that was Tory Patton.

"Ben…"

Sweat beaded along his back as she tightened her inner muscles around him. Damn, maybe he wasn't in charge after all. He slowly pulled back, so that only his tip remained inside her. He shifted his mouth to her other breast before thrusting deep inside her again.

He grabbed her hips and held her still when she would have met his thrust. She tightened herself around him again but this time he was ready for it.

"Lift you legs, babe. Bend them back to your body so I can get all the way inside you."

She did as he asked, and he slid all the way home. He buried his face against her neck, inhaling deeply the scent of his woman, and began to thrust slowly in and out of her body.

She gripped his buttocks, running her fingers lower until she gently scraped his sac with her fingernail. The feel of her touching him there made him boil.

He increased his spread until he felt her start to tighten around his body. She threw her head back and cried his name. He quickly covered her mouth with his and thrust deeper into her until his own orgasm rushed through him.

Breathing heavily, unable to move and unwilling to separate himself from her, Ben rested his head against her breast, tasting the sweat on her skin.

Her hands stroked up and down his back. He wanted to lie here forever and forget there was a dangerous world outside their bed, wanted to hold this fiery woman in his arms and do nothing but make love to her. He needed to cement their relationship so that he'd always have her waiting for him.

"Babe?"

She pinched his ass.

"Ouch."

"That's what I think every time you call me *babe*."

"Tory, sweetheart, you know I say it with love."

"Do you, Ben?"

He lifted himself up on his elbows and stared down into her wide eyes. "Yes, I do."

She smiled up at him. "We need to talk."

He wished he could read her gaze in the dim light but he couldn't, and what he heard in her voice concerned him.

Ben pulled her up onto his chest so that she could rest her head on his shoulder. She curved her body alongside his. He always held her this way. It made her feel safe, protected. Normally the feeling bothered her because she never wanted to be coddled, but tonight she liked it.

"Okay, what's up?" he asked, idly playing with a strand of her hair. He squeezed her so tightly she almost couldn't breathe. "God, I was scared tonight. Are you okay?"

Tears burned the back of her eyes and she hugged him back with the same intensity. She didn't know when or why, but Ben had carved a place for himself inside her.

She was so afraid to tell him about the baby and have him leave. Now that the moment was here, she didn't know if she could do it. "Um...something unexpected has come up."

"I hope this means you're leaving Berzhaan and going back to Manhattan."

"The story is here in Berzhaan," she said. But she *was* afraid to stay. Afraid that some of the risks she took—risks she'd always thought were worth it to get a good story—were going to harm her and her child…Ben's child.

"I'm not so sure," he said, loosening his grip on her and giving her a hard glare that she'd seen him use on his men.

"Are you trying to intimidate me?"

"Would that work?"

She shook her head. "Tell me more about the men that were captured in the alleyway."

"We interrogated them, but so far we haven't found any evidence they were involved in Andrea's kidnapping." He gave her a hard look. "They claim it was an attack of opportunity—they saw us and thought taking us hostage would make the Berzhaani government release Kemeni prisoners. It seems all the insurgents have hostages on the brain."

She shivered, and he held her closer. She didn't want to dwell on the fact that there was no way to avoid such dangers.

"I'm already making headway with the investigation," she said.

"You're a reporter, not a detective."

She thought about that. "I'm actually an anchorwoman."

"Then why are you in the field?"

She couldn't answer that, didn't want to have to say out loud that she'd been jealous of him and the adventures he was always on while she worked in the same city every day, even if it was New York. "I'm not sure. Especially now. I'm even more confused than before."

"Athena grad, that doesn't sound like you. Are you just tired, or still shaken up from almost dying?"

"Aren't you shook up?"

"Damn, woman, my hands are still shaking. I'm afraid to let go of you for a second because something else could go wrong and I might not react in time."

"Ben—"

"I know you can save yourself."

"Thank you." She meant the words, too. Ben always showed her respect even when his more primitive instincts told him to take over.

She didn't know where she was going yet. She knew that tonight she'd taken a huge risk with her life and the baby's that never would have bothered her before.

She sighed.

"What's the matter, Tory? Tell me. Trust me. Is it your job? That girl who's filling in for you isn't half the reporter you are."

She smiled at the way he defended her. "This isn't about work, Ben."

"What is it about?"

"Us."

He hugged her close and bent low to whisper in her ear. "Dammit, Tory. This better not be one of those good news/bad news situations where you make love to me and then ask if we can just be friends."

"It's not." She lifted her hand to his face, rubbing her fingers over the stubble on his jaw. He was always clean shaven and she knew that tonight getting to her had been his priority.

I'm pregnant, she thought. How hard could it be to just say those words out loud? "I had a physical before I came here."

"Is something wrong?" he asked, sitting up. She edged away from him. He skimmed his hands over her back, rubbing in soothing circles.

"No. God, I'm making a mess of this. I can't believe I make my living with words and now when I need them…"

"Babe, you're scaring the shit out of me. Tell me. Whatever it is, we can handle it together."

She reached over him, flicking on the bedside lamp because she had to look in his eyes when she told him. Wanted to see what his first reaction to the news would be.

She shifted around so that her legs were folded under her body and she was sitting up, looking down on Ben. She took his hand in hers, held it to her stomach and said, "We're going to have a baby."

He sat up and fell off the bed. Sat there on the floor staring up at her. She swallowed hard, unsure what to do.

"Ben?"

He pushed himself to his feet and put his hands on his hips, still just staring at her. He was totally naked, semihard and looked like an intimidating muscle man. But she stared into his eyes waiting for a sign. Something that would tell her what to do next.

"When did you find out?"

"Um…right before I got on the plane."

He took a deep breath. "First things first."

He moved back onto the bed and pulled her into his arms. And just held her against his chest. "Are you healthy? Are you okay? Do you need to have a doctor check you out after tonight?"

"I'm fine. I'm healthy, I'm going to see my OB/GYN as soon as I get back home."

"Which is going to be as soon as possible."

"Ben…"

"No. I'm not going to give in on this. You are going home where I know you aren't going to be running into terrorists or sleeper cells or anything like that."

"What about muggers?"

"They're all scared of you at home. Now sit back. I'm going to give you a lecture."

"You are?" She'd never seen this side of him before.

"I am. And you are going to listen to me and agree to never put yourself or our child in danger again."

"I agree."

He tilted his head. "What did you say?"

"You are absolutely right, I can't endanger our child's life. One of its parents needs to be safe."

Ben flushed and his hands clenched into fists. She felt guilty that she'd thrown those words out there but they were nothing less than the truth.

"What are you thinking?" she asked after several minutes had gone by.

"A million things," he said, his voice a hoarse whisper. He sank back on the bed next to her and wrapped his arms around her. He buried his face in her neck and she wondered if, like herself, he was reliving those moments earlier that could have gone wrong. If he were coming to terms with the fact that both their lives were dangerous.

"Oh, man, a baby."

She looked at him and saw a weird cocktail of emotions in his eyes—fear, excitement, nerves. It was a Ben Forsythe she'd never glimpsed before.

"I'm still trying to figure it out. To be honest, you caught me off guard. I thought we used protection every time."

She tilted her head to the side. When he got a call in the middle of the night to leave he often reached for her with a desperation and hunger that left room for nothing but the primitive bonding with her mate. No room for thought or consequences. "Not every time."

"That's right. We didn't just now, did we?"

"What do you think about this? I can't imagine us as parents, can you?" she asked, her secret fear. They were both so independent. How were they going to make room in their lives for a baby? How was she going to do it?

"I think you're going to be a great mom."

She wasn't so sure. She had absolutely no idea how to depend on anyone else, how to take care of anyone else. "Why?"

"Because you refuse to not be good at everything you try."

She smiled at the way he said it. "Okay, you might have a point. I think you'll be a good father."

"Not like my old man."

"What was your dad like?"

"Absent. Gone all the time."

Like Ben would be. His job wouldn't change, couldn't change just because she'd gotten pregnant. And everything that had been swirling around inside her suddenly bubbled up. "I'm going to have to stay in the anchor spot."

"Why?"

"Because I can't go after these kinds of stories if you're risking your life."

He scrubbed his hand over his face. "Let's not talk about that right now. I want to make love to the mother of my child."

"We can't ignore it forever, Ben."

"Not forever, but until I finish this mission and come home. I can't make decisions about this right now. I know that's not the manly way to be. But I almost lost you tonight, and that's hard enough for me to deal with."

She wasn't sure that was the right answer. Nothing had been settled, but she felt a lot lighter now that she'd shared her secret with him. Now that they both knew.

He shifted on the bed, rolling himself on top of her. She stared up into his slate-gray eyes and saw something there that made her wonder if they should have hashed this out further. But then he bent his mouth to hers and swept her up in a passion that left room for nothing other than the fire between them.

He held her under him, thrusting into her body, and she wrapped her arms and legs around him as they both crested together. She held him tightly to her, needing him in a way she'd never needed anyone else.

He reached out and turned off the light. She didn't really sleep that night, and when he got up in the pre-dawn light and dressed quietly, letting himself out of the room, she pretended she hadn't heard him.

Chapter 8

Tory's first day back in the New York office was no picnic. Yasmine, who'd filled in for her, had done a really good job. In fact, too good a job. Tyson was making noises like he wanted to keep the sub full-time, and Tory found herself in the middle of personal and career crises.

She'd heard nothing from Ben since he'd left their room in the middle of the night. Not knowing what else to do, she'd left him a voice mail about seeing his family over the Fourth of July weekend, which was only two days away. There was no way she could see them without Ben. Until she felt like the situation between the two of them was settled, she didn't want to involve either of their families.

Just because she'd been debating leaving the anchor desk didn't mean she was going to let some other reporter steal her show from her. When she left—*if* she left—it would be her own decision. Her show that first night back was on fire. She covered the latest on Andrea and the other hostages and had an exclusive interview with Andrea's mother and brother.

Afterward Tory returned to the newsroom and her desk. An interoffice envelope waited for her in the center of the desk, with a Post-it note from Cathy in research: *The books you requested.*

Tory opened them and saw *What to Expect When You're Expecting.* She slipped the book from the envelope and into her bag. That morning she'd started taking the vitamin her personal doctor had prescribed. She'd check the book out later.

She skimmed her e-mails. The phone rang and she reached for it.

"Patton."

"It's Ty. You're going to D.C. on the bullet train first thing in the morning. We're going to move your show to that studio for the time being."

"What's up?" she asked.

"Is Shawna at your desk yet?"

Tory glanced up and saw her producer walking toward her. Shawna's face was pale and she seemed angry and scared at the same time. "What's going on?"

Shawna entered Tory's office and closed the door. Tory pushed the hands-free button.

"We're both here," Shawna said. "What have you told Tory?"

"Just that you're both going to D.C."

"Why the sudden shift?" Tory asked.

"A severed fingertip was received at the Pentagon, addressed to the Joint Chiefs," Ty said. "It was Cobie McIntire's finger."

Tory felt the bile rise in the back of her throat. Oh, God. She closed her eyes trying to will the feeling of sickness away.

"Anything else?" she asked, trying to sound professional. What the hell kind of people did something like that?

"Just a reiteration to get our troops out of the Middle East before they are forced to take further action."

"Did the message specifically say 'our' troops?" she asked. Because if it had that could mean the terrorists were homegrown. "Has anyone claimed responsibility yet?"

"I have no goddamn idea what the message specifically said, Patton. You find out."

"I will, boss."

Shawna hit the disconnect button and leaned a hip against the desk. "My source says that a group called Freedom Now claimed responsibility when they sent the fingertip. They're a U.S.-backed militia group, determined to bring all troops home. Have you found any more leads on this case besides the woman who witnessed the abduction?"

"Some things, but they aren't coming together as quickly as I want them to. I do suspect there's a chance that Andrea may not have been the target. It could have been Shannon Conner."

"Shannon Conner? Why?"

"When I interviewed people in Suwan, I heard numerous references to 'that blond television news-woman.' Most didn't name Andrea. And they were both researching women's rights from different angles."

"What exactly was Shannon covering?"

"I have Cathy pulling the tapes for me."

"Sounds good. I asked our editors to analyze the footage the terrorists released so we can try to determine where they are being held. Authorities are being stingy with releasing info on the evidence, so we're doing what we can."

"Was a new tape or demands sent to the Joint Chiefs?"

"Yes. The network secured us a copy. The Pentagon

Spokesperson was foggy on the details when I called. Cobie's mom is the one who alerted my source."

Tory could only imagine how awful this time was for the woman as she waited for news on her son.

Shawna's cell phone rang and she moved out of Tory's office to take the call. Tory checked the headlines on the scanner and realized another Berzhaani military checkpoint had been hit by a suicide bomber yesterday evening.

When had the fingertip been sent? Was this a two-pronged offensive where they attacked the military and used the hostages to try to get them out of the area?

Shawna popped her head back into Tory's office. "I want to talk content for the show when we get to D.C."

"Okay. What'd you have in mind? I doubt we're going to get more than a canned statement from the military."

"You're right. But we do have Janice Petri, the founder of…" Shawna consulted her Blackberry and then glanced up. "Military Parents in Support of Withdrawal Now. She's issued a statement after the deaths earlier today at the military post and then mentioned the news-crew hostages."

Tory typed in the name of the organization while Shawna continued to brief her. She found the link to their Web site and bookmarked it for later. "Will she come into the studio?"

"Yes. But you'll have to tape the interview earlier in the day. She wouldn't come in for a live segment."

"No problem. I'll pull what I can on the group. Anything else?"

"I'm working on an aide from the Pentagon. I'm hoping to get someone who'll leak something or speak on promise of anonymity."

"I've got a few military contacts, I'll give it a try as well."

"Sounds good. I'll meet you at the train station in the morning."

Tory nodded as her producer left. She was concerned that the next communication they received from the terrorists would be the body of her friend. Closing her eyes, she pushed aside emotion and focused on the facts.

She looked up the contact information of a navy SEAL whom she'd helped to rescue last year, when she and Ben had met in Puerto Isla. Tom King had been presumed dead for several months before surfacing alive on the small Central American island. Tory had interviewed him when they'd finally gotten home safely, and over several days had gotten to know the man behind the story. She'd stayed in touch with him and his family ever since.

She e-mailed Tom, who tended to respond quickest to that form of communication.

Tom,
Hi. Have you heard of an organization called Military Parents in Support of Withdrawal Now? I'm doing an interview with their leader and would love to get your perspective on the group. You can reach me via e-mail or cell phone.
Tory.

Tory shut down her computer and gathered everything she'd need to work out of another office. She walked out of the newsroom, her mind focused on two developing stories—her own pregnancy and her missing friend.

Tory arrived in the nation's capital just before ten. She was surprised to find a courier waiting for her at the UBC studios with a key to Ben's Crystal City apartment and invitation to dinner with Alex. She tucked both things in her bag to deal with later.

Already the story was starting to come together. The new video they'd received from the terrorists showed the hostages in a desert. She'd left Ben a voice mail last night giving him that information. But the man was amazingly well-connected and more than likely hadn't needed her input.

"Welcome to the D.C. branch," Marcus Thompson said. He was in charge of this studio. He was a tall man of about sixty with blond hair and blue-green eyes. He'd been in the business forever. He was a master storyteller and Tory liked the man.

"This is the desk you'll be using while you're here, Tory. Shawna, I've put you there." He pointed. "If either of you need anything, let me know," Marcus said, and moved away from them.

Tory felt as if she were going to throw up. She'd read in her maternity book that not eating would make morning sickness worse. She reached into her bag and pulled out the bagel she'd stuffed in there last night.

"Hungry?" Shawna asked with a wry grin. This morning she was wearing what Tory thought of as her work uniform. Khaki pants, black shirt and a pair of tasseled loafers.

"Yes. Want half?" Tory asked. She wasn't normally a big eater but there had been an entire section of the book devoted to food.

She should call her sister-in-law for advice, except that Marie would probably alert her entire family to the news of the pregnancy.

"No. Roger fixed me breakfast before dropping me at the train station."

"Nice. I'm going to review my notes and see what my military contact had to say about the group that

Janice fronts and then get ready for the interview. She's coming here, right?"

Shawna consulted her PDA cell phone. "Yes, but not until two. I want you to go to the Pentagon and see what you can find."

"Who covers that for us?" Tory asked, making notes with one hand and carefully breaking off small pieces of the bagel with the other.

"Terrance Oppeli."

"I like him."

"You like everyone, Tory."

"Well, I don't know about that, but he and I were at NYU together."

"Good. See if you can find out more about the fingertip and what the note said. I'm going to check out the studio we'll be using for your show and make sure the background sets got here last night."

The Pentagon had released only the video showing the hostages bound and gagged and the note "Time is running out." The words had been written in Berzhaani, Russian and English. They'd lifted Cobie's hand and clearly showed the missing tip of his finger.

Just thinking about it made her feel sick and she swallowed hard, refusing to throw up this morning. Today she'd decided she was taking control of the pregnancy, and making it fit into her life. She took another bite of her bagel while searching for Terry's number. She found it and called him while logging onto the computer.

"This is Oppeli."

"Hey, Oppie! Tory Patton here. I need to talk to you about the Andrea Jancey story."

"What about it?" he asked, and added, "You know you're the only person who calls me Oppie anymore."

She pictured him in her mind. Oppie was slim and tall, a string bean of a man with bright red hair and freckles. He was a top-notch reporter and one of her oldest friends in the business.

"You were the one who insisted that would be your nickname."

"What was I thinking?" he asked, but she heard the laughter in his voice.

"Have you heard anything more from the Pentagon? Even unofficial would be fine. I'm not going to put the person on-air, I just need to make sure my story is going in the right direction."

"I'll see what I can find. They've been really closed-mouthed about this."

"Are any press conferences scheduled for this morning?" she asked.

"Nothing new, just routine updates on the troops in the Middle East."

"Save me a seat."

"You're coming?" he asked. "I don't think that you'll pick up anything I miss."

"Yes, Shawna wants me to dig around on the news-crew hostages."

"*Shawna* wants you to?"

Tory couldn't help laughing. "Okay, I want to."

"That's what I thought. You driving?"

"No."

"Then hurry up. In a cab you'll just make it."

"Thanks, Oppie."

"You're welcome, Patton."

She stood up too quickly and the nausea she'd been keeping at bay swamped her. She hoped she'd make it to the restroom. Where the hell *was* the restroom? She ran into the hall and found the closest one. She barely made it to the stall before she threw up.

When she came out there were two women standing at the sink. "Are you okay?"

"I think I ate some bad fish last night," Tory said. She washed her hands and face before leaving the bathroom and hurrying to catch a cab. Her mind wasn't on the story though. Her mind was on the fact that she was going to have to go public with her pregnancy pretty soon. Shawna was going to realize what was going on.

Tory rubbed the back of her neck, not ready for

that conversation. Not ready to let anyone else in on something she was still coming to terms with herself.

Ben heard Tory on his voice mail and panicked for a second. He knew he shouldn't have left the way he had but there was too much to talk about and he needed his head in the warrior game right now. He wanted to be in action, fighting for his life, no time to think of anything but his men and his duty.

Her message informed him of the new tape and the fingertip the Pentagon had received. He already had that intel from his CO, but he appreciated the fact she'd called. She didn't say anything else. He should have felt relieved, but didn't.

They'd searched every damned inch of Suwan, so he hadn't been surprised to learn that the hostages were now in the desert. Ben waited on the street corner in Sovetski near the newsstand where he'd encountered Tory. He'd had a call this morning from Kambiz, who had some information for him.

He'd brought only O'Neill with him and the other man was backing him up from across the street.

Kambiz and his men had been searching for information in their neighborhood and Ben was anxious to learn what the man had found.

"Do you see your man yet?" O'Neill asked.

"Negative. Why?"

"There's some action down the street. Looks like a police raid."

"Direction?"

"Your right."

Ben nonchalantly glanced in the direction that O'Neill had indicated. From his position it was difficult to make out exactly what was going on. But O'Neill was watching the street through high-powered binoculars.

"I'll check it out."

"I've got you covered."

"Salvo, are you listening?" Ben asked, suspecting their team member would be monitoring them even though he hadn't been asked to.

"Yes, sir."

"What have you got on the police frequency?"

"Definite activity. I don't speak Berzhaani well enough to tell you exactly what they're saying, but I have one of the other guys translating. I'll keep you posted."

Ben walked down the street, using the groups of pedestrians for cover until he reached the block where the police cars were parked in front of a fifteen-story apartment building.

"Got anything yet, Salvo?"

"They had a report of three dead bodies on the fourteenth floor. A small one-bedroom apartment."

"Could this have anything to do with our mission?" Ben asked. The fact that the police were raiding an apartment near where Golshon had seen the abductions made him want to check it out.

"I'm not sure," Salvo said.

Ben wiped the sweat running down the back of his neck. It was early afternoon and hotter than hell. "Can you see any activity in the interior of the building?"

O'Neill responded. "Negative, sir. I'm moving for a better angle."

"Salvo?"

"Yes, sir. Okay, we've secured clearance for you to be at the sight. Identify yourself and you can enter."

Ben approached the officer at the front of the building. He identified himself and went upstairs to survey the room. There were five men securing the crime scene. Ben stood in the doorway knowing that he'd contaminate the room if he entered it.

"Can I help?" the officer at the door asked.

"I'm from the U.S. embassy. I'd like to speak to the officer in charge." Ben's team was never officially associated with the military.

"One moment." The man left him at the door and Ben was surprised to see Kambiz walking toward him.

"I'm the officer in charge. Sorry I was late for our meeting."

"No problem, I didn't realize you were law enforcement the other night."

"I'm a lieutenant with the Suwan police force. I've been working the hostage case. I'm sorry for not clarifying that the other night. I've been working with our undercover officers and felt the less said, the better."

"I'm with the U.S. military."

"I thought so. I think you'll be interested in these men. They are the ones who took the Americans."

"Why are you showing me this?" Ben asked, surveying the scene, taking in as many details as he could.

Kambiz reached into his pocket. "Because I think this belongs to one of yours."

Ben glanced down at the other man's hand. In his palm was a man's slim brown leather wallet. Inside were a press card and a diplomat badge from the U.S. embassy in Suwan. The picture on the identification card was Paul Manning's. Kambiz was sharp.

"Can I keep this?"

"It's evidence so I'll need it back."

"I'll return it. We need to verify the authenticity."

"I understand."

"Did you find anything else?"

"No." The terse answer spoke volumes for Kambiz's frustration.

"Did you interview the neighbors?"

"Yes. They saw and heard nothing."

Too bad Tory had gone back to Manhattan. Ben was positive she could have gotten some of the neighbors to talk.

"Thanks," Ben said, taking the wallet and leaving the building.

O'Neill waited for him on the street.

"Is this Paul's?" Ben asked, tossing the wallet to O'Neill.

He opened it and looked at the ID card. "Near as I can tell."

"That's what I thought." Ben scanned the area, looking for something, someone they could talk to. They were trained for action and interrogation, not interviewing civilians.

"They were in this building. We know they've been moved because of the new hostage tape. Why are the three men who kidnapped the Americans dead up there?"

"A falling out?" O'Neill suggested as they walked back toward their vehicle.

That was one theory. "I'd feel a lot more comfortable with this situation if we knew more about this Freedom Now group."

"Salvo is working on that."

"Let's work the street, see if we can find someone

who saw anyone entering or exiting with the hostages."

O'Neill nodded and started toward a grocery store on the left side of the street. Ben doubled back to the Internet café on the right. This was the frustrating part of his job. The part that he hated the most. Searching for information and coming up empty.

Today it was doubly so, because he had that feeling in his gut that he was missing something. That the evidence he was searching for was right in front of him and he couldn't see it.

Chapter 9

The set for Tory's show, *A Closer Look,* was set up much like an afternoon talk show. No typical anchor desk—she usually stood in the middle of the set to deliver news or talk to reporters in the field. On the occasions when she had an in-studio guest, such as Janice Petri, they used an armchair and love seat. There was a coffee table that they had coffee cups set on.

Janice was fifty-two but looked younger. She was very slim and chic looking, reminding Tory of Ben's mother. Her blond hair was perfectly coiffed and she wore a DKNY pants suit and designer Italian pumps. She made Tory feel like a hick from a ranch in central Florida instead of the seasoned professional she was.

Tory shook that feeling off and glanced down at her notes, waiting for her cue to start. As soon as she was given it, she smiled at the camera.

"Today on *A Closer Look* we are pleased to have Janice Petri in the studio. Janice is the founder and president of Military Parents in Support of Withdrawal Now, an action group formed by parents whose children are serving in military action around the world. Welcome, Janice."

"Thanks for inviting me to speak with you today, Tory."

"How was this organization born?" she asked. Janice leaned forward in her chair, a pensive look on her face.

"It was born in my living room after a support group meeting for parents who'd lost children overseas."

Tory didn't have to glance down at her notes. She remembered the details of Janice's son's death. "This was last fall, after your youngest son, Alan, was killed in action?"

"Yes, it was. It was such a blow to lose him." There was a sheen of tears in Janice's eyes but she didn't start to cry.

Tory directed the conversation away from that time. She didn't like it when her guests were too emotional on the show because then she felt as if she'd gone too far in the interview. She wanted honest feelings, but not a total breakdown. "What branch of the military was Alan in?"

"The Marines."

"As was your husband, Rodney?"

"My ex-husband, yes and our other son, Rick, is still over there."

"Tell me more about your organization," Tory said.

"While we were talking about our children and what they'd believed, why they'd joined the military, we realized that none of them wanted to be a part of a military action that had no possible positive outcome."

"What do you mean by positive outcome?" Tory asked. She'd been to the group's Web site, but their mission statement had focused only on military withdrawal from the Middle East.

"Just that the fighting in that part of the world has gone on since the beginning of recorded time and it still continues. Our kids are dying over there and so far nothing has changed."

"So you decided to form a political action group?" Tory asked.

"Yes. But we started with a letter-writing campaign. Bebe Pennybaker created a Web site for us and we invited everyone we knew through our children to join."

"How does your ex-husband feel about the organization, since he was career military?"

"He hasn't been too happy about it as a retired staff sergeant, but as a father he can understand why I need to do this."

There were complex layers to Janice Petri, layers that Tory wasn't sure she was getting to. "Janice, you released a statement when the hostages were taken saying that your organization had warned that it would only be a matter of time until Americans were taken hostage. What kind of action do you think could have prevented this?"

"A total pullout from the area or at least a partial one."

"Have you heard of a group called Freedom Now? They have claimed responsibility for taking the hostages."

"Yes. They obviously aren't interested in a peaceful solution to the problem like we are."

"What do you know about them?"

"Only what I've heard on the news."

"Wrap it up," Shawna said in Tory's earpiece.

"Thank you for being with us today, Janice, and for talking to us about Military Parents in Support of Withdrawal Now. I hope you'll come back again."

They closed the interview and Tory walked Janice off the set. As they left the studio, Janice was quiet.

"Thanks for talking to me," Tory said.

"You're welcome. When will this show air?"

"Tonight."

"Great, thanks."

Janice left and Tory made her way back to her temporary desk. She had a voice mail waiting and dialed in to retrieve it.

"It's Alex. Are you and Ben in town? How about dinner tonight? Call me."

Alex worked for the FBI crime lab. They'd been in the same orientation group at Athena Academy for girls, the Cassandras, and Tory thought of her as a sister. But the reality was, Alex was *Ben's* sister.

She returned Alex's call and got her voice mail. "Hey, Alex. I'm so sorry, I can't make dinner tonight. I'm in the middle of a story. I'll call you when I have some free time. I'm not sure where your stubborn brother is, but I'll tell him you're looking for him next time we talk."

She hung up and checked her e-mail. There was a return message from Tom King, which she opened immediately.

I know very little about Military Parents in Support of Withdrawal Now, but I think the group was founded after a father tried to kill himself and the

officers delivering the news of his son's death.
The man's name is Larry Maxwell.
—Tom

Tory clicked over to the Internet and did a Google
search on Larry Maxwell. She came up with a few
hits of the same story. She remembered the incident
as soon as she read the AP article.

Tory didn't know if talking to Maxwell would
reveal anything further or not. She continued reading
articles on the Internet and found one that gave her
the link she'd been looking for. Janice's ex-husband
and Larry had served together in the Marines. Larry
had retired after only two tours, but Rodney Petri had
stayed on.

There was a picture of a Veteran's Day celebration from three years ago, a Main Street parade that
showed Janice and Rodney Petri along with Larry
Maxwell and his wife, Alice.

She searched for Freedom Now and found a Web
site with a message to the U.S. President and the
Joint Chiefs. They had two pictures of the hostages.
The newest one showed Cobie's hand, one fingertip
missing. *Sick.* Tory forwarded the link to Jay
Matthews for input. Jay knew the landscape in Berzhaan
better than she did. Maybe he could pinpoint where
they were based on the tape.

She searched through Lexis/Nexis and an Internet phone book until she found a contact number for Larry. She dialed the number.

"I'm not here, leave a message." The voice was gruff and not exactly inviting.

Tory put on her best upbeat voice. "Hi, Mr. Maxwell, this is Tory Patton with UBC television. I'm interested in talking to you about a story I'm working on."

Tory went through the list of other major players in Military Parents in Support of Withdrawal Now and left messages for Bebe Pennybaker and Melanie Wilkins. Those two women, along with Janice Petri, were the ones who ran the organization and took care of the daily details.

Tory investigated parents who'd lost children in the military and lined up interviews with those who supported the U.S. military action in the Middle East and Berzhaan.

These stories gave her a legitimate reason to poke around the Pentagon and see what she could uncover about the hostages.

Russ wasn't happy. The media was talking to Janice Petri, the government was ignoring them and the kid whose fingertip they'd cut off was showing signs of infection. He put the word out through the

Freedom Now network to find a medic, but the only person to respond was a man that he hadn't met. Russ didn't know if they could trust him.

Larry was looking nervous and a little afraid. Jake and Rodney were on sentry duty, patrolling the perimeter around his hunting cabin in Arizona. Leaving Berzhaan had been difficult despite their car bomb decoy, and they'd been forced to kill the men who'd helped them kidnap the news crew. He still couldn't believe those idiots had encouraged others to try to kidnap yet another reporter.

"That kid doesn't look good. What if the infection spreads and kills him?" Larry asked. He'd just finished administering an injection of a sedative they were using to keep all of the hostages unconscious.

"Then he'll be our first victim," Russ said, but his gut churned at the thought of another dead son.

"What the hell is wrong with the president?" Larry asked. "Does he really want three more deaths on his hands? On the hands of his administration?"

"You know he doesn't give a fuck about the common man or the loss of his children."

Larry paled, and Russ guessed it was because his son had been in a Special Forces unit and had met President Gabriel Monihan. Larry had actually received a kind personal letter from the man when Garret had died.

"I think I can get a nurse to come out here."

"No one can know this location."

"Russ, he's moaning in his sleep. I can't—"

"Yes, you can. We can't change anything at this time. We have to keep moving forward."

Larry nodded. "I've got to go home and feed my dogs."

Larry lived just outside of Phoenix, in Palmer Junction, on a sprawling ranch. Russ wasn't too sure that Larry wouldn't try to nab some kind of medical personnel to bring out here.

"Don't bring anyone else out here," he warned again.

"I heard you the first time," Larry said.

"Make sure you listen. I don't want to have to kill any more than the three in there."

Larry nodded. "I'll be back in an hour, maybe less. You need anything?"

"No."

Russ had stocked the hunting cabin so they'd be ready for a long haul. Larry left, and Russ sat down on a folding chair and watched the three young people who were bound, gagged and all propped against the wall.

They smelled of perspiration and urine. Each day they allowed them to come off the sedative for a brief amount of time to drink a vitamin-filled shake. Then they were sedated again.

Russ rubbed the back of his neck. This was the damned last thing he'd ever imagined himself doing. But desperation had ways of changing a man.

The cameraman moaned and Russ went over to him and checked the finger. It was hot to the touch, swollen and throbbing.

Russ wasn't ready to kill any of their hostages.

What was he going to do?

Only when the other men were gone did he feel this…fear that he'd made a bad decision. In front of his men, he remained their leader, fearless in the course they were on.

He pulled back from the kid and walked around the room trying to figure out what move to take next. The kid was getting worse and Larry was right, something needed to be done. He went to his laptop and pulled up the list of men who had joined Freedom Now to see what there was to know about the medic—Bill Jones. Although he'd corresponded with Bill on the Internet several times, Russ just couldn't tell if Bill would appreciate the extreme measures that he, Larry, Jake and Rodney had deemed necessary for their cause.

He radioed Rodney and Jake. "Either of you know Bill Jones well enough to vouch for him?"

"Why?" Rodney asked.

"We need a medic."

"I've never met the man but I can put out some feelers. It could take a few days to get an affirmative."

"Jake?"

"Same."

Russ signed off and leaned back against the wall. He didn't want another hostage, but if they brought the medic here and he balked at what they'd done, they could overpower him and sedate him like the other hostages.

Either way it raised the chance of a kill, but he'd started this operation determined to do whatever was necessary to see it through, and that was exactly what he still intended to do. It seemed somehow fitting to be taking this stand so close to the Fourth of July. All for Tommy.

Fatigue weighed on Tory's body as she walked down the hallway toward Ben's fourteenth-floor condo. She'd spent the last hour of the day instant messaging with Jay, who'd found an irregularity in the tape of the hostages. Her back hurt, her feet hurt and she wanted to sleep for a long time.

She put her key in Ben's door and pushed it open. Alex Forsythe sat on the couch.

Maybe it was exhaustion, or maybe she just had

danger on the brain, but as soon as she saw Alex, Tory thought something must have happened to Ben. Her head felt tight and spots moved in front of her eyes. Alex stood up and walked toward her. Tory could see her mouth moving but she couldn't hear the words.

She closed her eyes, trying to force the blackness to recede but it didn't. Everything went totally black and she slumped to the floor.

When she opened her eyes, Alex was crouched over her, checking her pulse.

"Lie still. You fainted, Tory."

"I never faint. How could that happen?" she asked. "Why are you here, Alex?"

"Mother, Grandpa Charles and I want to take you to dinner. We're also having a barbecue tomorrow, if you're free. Justin will be there."

Ben was safe. Tory closed her eyes as tears threatened to fall. If she started crying Alex would know something more was wrong. Tory had to get hold of herself.

Alex propped two pillows under Tory's feet. For a second Tory wanted to confess everything to her friend. To share the burden of her worry about the baby and what that would mean to her career. Her worry about Andrea and the other hostages and the fear that she was missing something every time she reviewed those tapes. Her worry that Ben might be hurt somewhere and she'd never know about it until his body was flown home for a funeral.

"You couldn't just call?" she said, hoping she sounded sassy and not as if she were whining.

"I came over to ask you because you can never turn down a personal invitation."

Tory flushed. It was true, she had no problem leaving messages to decline, but face-to-face, she couldn't do it unless she had a legitimate reason. Which she didn't. She only wanted to avoid Ben's family until she and Ben had come to some sort of agreement about the baby and their lives together.

"I'm working on a story that just won't quit."

"I know you, you probably haven't eaten at all today." Her eyes narrowed. "In fact, that's probably why you fainted."

Alex did know her. "Okay, do I have time to shower and change?"

"Are you feeling okay? Honestly, if you're sick, I'll help you get to bed and check in tomorrow."

"I'm fine. You're right, I haven't been eating properly and I've been sitting in the edit bay all day searching for something that I may have missed on those hostage tapes. Talking to you and your grandfather may be just what I need. Although your mother's another story. She's scary."

Tory sat up and Alex put her hand on Tory's shoulder. "Don't rush. Take your time getting up."

"I'm fine, really."

Alex sighed. "You are too stubborn."

"Hello pot, it's the kettle calling."

Alex laughed and Tory smiled. There wasn't a woman among the Cassandras who wasn't stubborn.

"What's going on with the search for that black-mailer, A?"

Alex widened her eyes. "Come to dinner and I'll fill you in."

"All right. For that, I'll rally."

Tory started to stand and Alex rose with her. "We're going to have dinner at Mother's favorite restaurant." She rolled her eyes.

"You look casual."

"I'm going home to change. You know Mother doesn't eat in casual places."

No, Veronica wouldn't. "She does have an image to think about."

Alex made a face at her. "Are you going to be okay if I leave?"

"I've been showering and getting dressed on my own for years."

"Yes, but you've never blacked out before."

"I feel a lot better already." That was true. Now

that she knew Ben was okay, or at least not deceased or severely injured, she was fine.

"Eight-thirty at Romanos. Don't call to cancel once I leave. I'm going to answer every call that comes in on my cell and house phone."

"I can't cancel now unless the station calls me in."

"That's right."

"Thanks, Alex," Tory said as her friend walked to the door.

"Any time."

Alex left and Tory pulled out her Blackberry, scrolling through the stored numbers until she found her OB/GYN's. She dialed the office, but they were closed for the day and she had to be connected through the service to the doctor on call.

"This is Dr. Miller."

"This is Tory Patton, I'm a patient of Dr. Franz's. I'm pregnant, about six weeks along, and I just fainted."

"What were you doing?"

"Entering my condo."

She confirmed that she hadn't eaten much and that she had been under stress. He told her in a firm voice to eat something and take it easy, and to call back immediately if she felt any cramping. But more than likely, she was just fine.

She grabbed a health-food bar from the pantry and went into the bedroom. Ben's bed. She laid down on his side—the right—and closed her eyes. His scent was on the bed clothes and she wrapped her arms around his pillow and buried her face in the downy softness.

She just breathed, trying not to relive the fear she'd felt when she'd seen Alex. She really needed to hear Ben's voice but she was afraid to call him. Afraid if she heard him, she'd break down and beg him to come home.

She sat up as she realized that she needed him. That right now, she wanted his arms around her. She'd never needed anyone except her parents.

Was needing Ben a bad thing? She didn't know. He needed to stay focused on his mission. He didn't need to hear how afraid she was that he might not make it back.

She hurried through her shower. When she got out she saw she'd missed a call on her cell phone. It was from Shawna.

Tory finished dressing and getting ready before calling her producer. Alex was never going to believe her if she did have to leave to go to a live shoot.

"Hey, Shawna, what's up?"

"Nothing urgent. I wanted to let you know we finally got through to Larry Maxwell. He's some kind of wealthy recluse. He'll talk to you, but only if you come to Arizona."

"Why? Did you tell him we could do a satellite uplink?"

"Yes, but he was insistent you'd be there in person. I checked your schedule and saw you're scheduled for two days near Phoenix for some Athena Academy event."

"Yes, the dedication of the new science wing. I'm speaking. But if we get a break in Andrea's story, I'll have to miss it." Alex would be there, she could take Tory's place.

"I think you should go and interview Larry Maxwell while you're there. Cathy in research thinks she found a tie between Larry and Freedom Now."

"What kind of tie?"

"She's e-mailing you the documents. But it seems that he was pretty active on their chat room and message boards until about six months ago."

Tory felt a tingling in her gut. The kind she always had when she was on to something big. "This is it. The break we've been looking for. I'll come back to the station—"

"No, Patton, you won't. We'll work on this tomorrow. The world won't end if you take a few hours off."

Chapter 10

Dinner with Ben's family would be very warm and welcoming. Tory had known them through Alex for years. Their grandfather Charles had been one of the founders of the Athena Academy. Their mother, Veronica, though truly a scary matriarch of D.C. society, had even warmed up to Tory after Tory had been instrumental in saving Ben's life a year and a half ago. Never mind that he'd been in danger because of Tory.

Tory called Alex on her cell phone when she arrived and Alex came out to meet her. "You look a lot better."

"Thanks. I feel better, too. I've been working really hard on the story."

"I know." Alex squeezed Tory's hand before leading her through the restaurant.

Tory saw several of her colleagues when she entered and they waved at her as she walked past with Alex.

"Is Justin here with you?"

"No. He's working tonight. He'll join us tomorrow for the Fourth. We're having a barbecue, remember?"

Alex looked happy when she talked about Justin. More than happy. Her eyes warmed with an inner glow that Tory had never seen in her friend before she'd met her FBI colleague.

They had been given a small, private dining area in the back of the restaurant. A round table graced the middle of the elegant room. The walls were lined with wine bottles. Charles Forsythe stood when they entered, giving Tory a hug in greeting.

Veronica greeted her with a smile, but Tory stopped in shock when she saw the other person at the table. *Ben.* When had he gotten back? Why hadn't he called her? Why wasn't *he* at his condo?

"Surprise," he said.

She glanced at Alex. "Is this why you were so insistent I come out tonight?"

"Maybe."

Tory turned up her on-air smile when she really

wanted to pull Ben aside and force him to tell her what was going on.

"Grandpa, Mother, Alex, please excuse Tory and me for a moment."

Ben put his hand under her elbow and led her out of the private dining room and down a hallway to the small alcove leading to the bathrooms.

He wrapped one arm around her waist and pulled her close and she struggled to remember that she didn't know where she stood with Ben. Struggled to remain indifferent.

She pushed against his chest. "Why didn't you call me?"

"There wasn't time. Alex mentioned she'd invited you to dinner, so I thought I'd surprise you. Don't worry, I already told the family we can't make the barbecue tomorrow."

"Ben, I know this isn't a good time, but, why did you leave me like you did in the hotel?"

He clenched his jaw. "There are some things I just don't know how to handle."

"What things? We're talking about a baby," she said, keeping her voice low, and remembering that she was in a public place and that she was a well-known anchorwoman. She couldn't afford to do anything to jeopardize her on-air image.

Ben took her hand. "I'm an ass."

She wanted to smile at the way he said it. But she couldn't let him off the hook yet. "Go on, I'm listening."

He threw his head back and laughed, and she felt her stomach clench. God, she missed this man. She leaned up on tiptoe and took his mouth in a deep kiss. "We don't want to keep your family waiting."

"I don't care about my family right now, Tory. I care about you."

"That's sweet," she said.

"Not sweet, true. I've been thinking about you and the baby, and I've come to a decision."

She held her breath and hated that. Whatever decision Ben made, she'd survive, but she was honest enough to admit she wanted the father of her child by her side. She needed Ben in ways she couldn't even vocalize, didn't ever want to.

"And that decision is?"

"Damn, babe, that sounds so cold."

She realized she was using her on-air breathing techniques to keep her voice calm and her emotions at bay. "I'm anything but cold about this Ben. I just can't afford to be…"

"Emotional in public," he said at last. "My timing sucks today."

"Oh, I don't know about that. Seeing you was a very nice surprise."

"Very nice? That's it?"

"That's not a bad thing, Ben. We should be getting back to your family."

She turned to lead the way back to the table but he stopped her with a hand on her shoulder. "Tory?"

"Yes?"

He cleared his throat. "Will you marry me?"

Her jaw dropped, and she might have gasped. Air suddenly seemed scarce. She took three steps back to him so that there was no space between their bodies. She pressed her hands on his chest, trying to force him back into the shadows where they could have more privacy. In his eyes, she read determination and something else she couldn't define.

"Well?" he asked, impatiently.

"I'm thinking about it. To be honest I'd love to marry you but I'm not sure that's the correct decision."

"Why not? I've asked you, you want to say yes. As far as I'm concerned, it's a done deal."

She shook her head. "I wish that it were so simple. But we have to think of the future. We both crave excitement and work in jobs that take us around the world. We scarcely have a normal routine. What kind of marriage would we have?"

"One where we both love each other. One where we can depend on each other."

"How could I depend on you, Ben? I don't even know if you'll be in the country when I give birth."

"I'll take leave, Tory. Don't make my job an excuse."

She bit her lower lip and turned away. Was she doing that? Was she projecting the fears she had for Ben's safety onto his career to give her a reason to ask him to quit?

She rubbed her head. "I'm really not sure we should have this discussion here. I'll consider your proposal."

He cupped the back of her neck, lowering his head to hers. "You do that."

He kissed her, then took her hand and directed her back to the private dining room and his family. Throughout dinner, she kept up with the conversation on one level, but deep inside of herself she was overwhelmed by the fact that Ben had asked her to marry him, and she wasn't sure if she should say yes or not.

Tory looked thinner than the last time he'd seen her and as they entered his condo after dinner, he realized he needed to find out more about her pregnancy. He was in D.C. for a morning meeting at the Pentagon, and he should be preparing for that, but he couldn't rest until he settled things with Tory.

He wasn't going to back off until she agreed to be his wife. He needed that. For the first time he could remember, he really needed to have his personal life settled.

They both removed their shoes and left them by the front door.

"You look determined."

"I am."

"I'm tired, Ben. Being pregnant is taking a toll on my body. I know I can find a way to cope with the fatigue, but so far, there hasn't been time."

He smiled to himself. Of course, she would "figure out" pregnancy and would be an ultra-efficient model of what an expectant mother could be. Tory was a dynamo and the love he felt for her hit him in the gut.

He almost started sweating, realizing that she hadn't agreed to be his wife and she could walk out that door whenever she wanted. She could leave him and he'd have to let her go. Even though every instinct he possessed would scream for him to keep her by his side—by whatever means necessary.

"Have you started reading any books?"

"A couple. But we got a lead on the hostages tonight, and I've been concentrating on that."

"Do you have to work tonight?" he asked, glancing at the clock. It was after ten but he knew

Tory functioned on about six hours sleep, so for her it was still early in the evening.

"Actually, Shawna told me to take the night off."

"Which is why you asked Grandfather about his connections at the Pentagon."

"The conversation was going that way," she said.

Ben smiled. The conversation had gone that way because Tory had brought it there after hearing the latest on Alex and Allison Gracelyn's search for the mysterious "A" and Sam St. John and her twin sister's, Elle's, dangerous adventures in Greece. The Cassandras just couldn't stay out of trouble.

He wanted to laugh but didn't. She walked into the bedroom and then into the attached bathroom, flicking on the light and starting to remove her makeup. Ben followed her, leaning against the wall to just watch her.

It was a very private thing for a man to witness. Tory moved around his bathroom, looking very at home there, and in his gut the tightness that had lingered when she hadn't immediately said yes to his proposal started to lessen.

"I have a meeting at the Pentagon in the morning."

She raised one eyebrow, meeting his gaze in the mirror. "Can I come?"

She finished washing her face and started brushing her teeth. He joined her at the sink. "No, you may not. But if you're good, I'll share my intel with you."

They both finished with their teeth and Tory moved into the walk-in closet to change out of her clothing. She unbuttoned her blouse, tipping her head to one side. "Define good?"

He unbuttoned his shirt and tossed it into the hamper. "You could start by agreeing to marry me."

"That's bribery." She slowly unzipped her pants and pushed them to her feet before shrugging out of her blouse and standing in front of him in her matching bra and panties.

"Yes, it is," he said, his voice gruff with need. His body hardened. He reached down, unfastened his pants and pushed them over his hips and off.

"Conduct unbecoming an officer, Bennington. Whatever would your superiors say?"

"I'd explain that you drove me to it. That you wouldn't agree to marry the father of your child unless I applied pressure."

"You'd say that to them?" she asked, unfastening her bra and letting the satiny garment fall down her arms.

"Only if you brought charges against me," he said, walking to her and lifting her by her waist. "Let's negotiate now so that it doesn't come to a formal inquiry."

He lifted her until her breasts were level with his mouth and he suckled her. She moaned, her hands clasping his head, her legs wrapping around his waist.

He carried her back to the bed and lowered them both on top of the comforter. He skimmed his hands over her body, caressing her to find any changes their child had made to it. His mouth followed the path of his hands, arousing them both to a fever pitch.

Her hands roamed over his body, bringing him quickly to the boiling point. He settled himself between her legs, held her wrists in both of his hands above her head.

He rubbed his chest against her breasts, reveling in the feel of her tight nipples against his skin. "This is so right, babe."

She twisted her hands in his and captured his wrists. She levered herself up and bit at his lower lip. "Don't toy with me, Ben. Make love to me. I want to feel that you really are home."

He shifted his body and slid into hers. He kept his strokes shallow, drawing out the anticipation in his body and in her. She shifted under him trying to draw him deeper but he waited until her movements were almost frantic before driving deeply into her body.

He groaned at the feeling of rightness that shook him. The back of his spine tingled and he realized he was closer to the edge than he'd thought. She tightened her inner muscles around his erection and he tensed, breathing deeply to hold off his orgasm. He needed to bring her pleasure first.

He slid his hand between their bodies, caressed her between her legs until she moaned his name and climaxed under him. He held her hips, thrusting into her only three more times before he came. He rocked between her legs until they'd both ridden out their orgasm. Then he collapsed next to her on the bed and pulled her into his arms.

"This thing between us isn't going away, Tory. We are meant to be together. Why won't you say yes?"

She swallowed hard and met his gaze. "I need time to think this through. I'm still dealing with being pregnant."

"How much time?"

"A few days."

He could give her that. But for his sanity and job performance, he needed an answer before he went back into the field.

Tory entered the newsroom and was surprised to see Jay Matthews waiting at her desk. He leaned one hip against it and casually sipped his coffee.

"Morning, Jay. Happy Fourth of July. When did you get back?" she asked.

"Last night. I'm on vacation for a week."

"Then why are you here?"

He shrugged. "I figured if you and I put our heads together, we might be able to figure out what's off with that last hostage tape."

"Thanks, Jay. That sounds great. Let me grab a cup of coffee and then we can get started."

"I'll meet you in the edit bay."

Tory fixed herself a cup of decaf and headed down the hall to the edit suite. She entered the low-lit room. Jay glanced up as she entered.

"I found something in that tape that you might be interested in."

"What?"

"Come over here and I'll show you."

"You can't just tell me?"

"I could, but then you wouldn't realize how brilliant I am."

She waited while he pulled up the most recent tape they had of Andrea and the other hostages.

"Watch here," he said, pointing to a window that was only partially visible at regular magnification. Jay zoomed in and stilled the frame, and she realized that the landscape looked familiar to her and not at all like the Berzhaan desert.

"Where is it?"

"Near as I can tell, Arizona or New Mexico," Jay

said. He pointed out several plants that were specific to those states. "What convinced me was the next few frames."

He played the tape at a slow speed and Tory saw why he was convinced that they were in a desert area of the U.S. There was a gila monster sunning itself on a rock. That combined with the landscape, made her feel certain that Jay was correct.

Excitement churned in her gut. She searched her memory from her time at Athena Academy, which was situated outside of Phoenix. This type of landscape seemed similar. "Can you scan the landscape, find us something else to go on? I can scout areas, but the desert is immense and I need something solid to go on."

"I'll try, but we're limited by what's actually on the film and I'm not an editor. Phil's meeting me here later and we're going to analyze the film frame by frame."

"Good idea. Why don't you have him go over the interior, too, and see if you can find something…a map, a paper, anything that will narrow down where they are. What kind of building do you think it is?"

Jay shrugged and zoomed back out. "I have no idea."

"Whoever shot this isn't a professional. Look at how the film jiggles when he shifts."

"I noticed that. Also, he zooms in and out in a really rough way."

"Maybe he filmed something he shouldn't have."

"If he did, I intend to find it."

"I'll be in the office after I tape my show. Then I'm flying to Athena Academy for a dedication of a new wing. If we're right, and this is Arizona or New Mexico, I'll practically be right there."

"I've got your numbers. I'll keep you posted on what I find."

"I thought you were on vacation?"

"We're in the twenty-four-hour news business, Patton, we are never fully on vacation."

"Thanks, Jay," she said before leaving him to work.

She walked back to her desk and checked her e-mail. She had two messages from Bebe Pennybaker with some more statistics on the parents group and a schedule of their upcoming rallies. Tory made a note of the information. The next rally wasn't until the end of July.

Her phone rang. "UBC. This is Tory Patton."

"Hey, it's Shawna. Did you get the packet I left you from research about Maxwell?"

"I'm getting to it now."

"It's almost nine o'clock, Patton."

"I know the time. I was just in the edit bay with Jay. He found some interesting things on that last tape."

"Like?"

"Like they are almost definitely in the U.S. somewhere."

"That makes sense. The group has to be based here."

"Jay's working with Phil to see if they can get more detail on the location."

"Did you talk to Terrance this morning?"

"No, why?"

"There were several high-level meetings going on at the Pentagon today, all of them closed sessions that the Secretary of Defense wouldn't comment on."

"What kind of meetings? Are they giving the appearance of at least thinking about withdrawing troops?"

"It sounds that way. I'll be in the office in a few minutes. Can you meet me at ten to discuss today's show?"

"Sure."

Shawna disconnected and Tory opened the packet from research, reading the literature and making notes for her interview with Larry Maxwell. The man had served two tours in Vietnam and then came home to run the ranch that had been in his family for generations. He'd married a local woman and had three kids. The oldest son had been killed nine months earlier in Iraq. Tory looked at the picture of Larry Maxwell from the AP wire.

It had been taken after he'd tried to kill himself and the officers who'd delivered the news of his son's death. The man in that photo looked desperate and grieved. Tory's stomach clenched in sympathy.

Chapter 11

Being back at Athena Academy brought a rush of memories to Tory. As she walked the halls, she wondered for the first time if the baby she carried was a girl. Maybe she'd be part of the next generation of Athena grads to conquer the world.

She was at Athena today to dedicate a new wing in the memory of her friend and mentor, Lorraine Miller. Rainy, as they'd called her, had been several years older than Tory and Alex and their group of friends, the Cassandras. Rainy had been their group leader and mentor during their first year.

Almost two years ago, Rainy had died under sus-

picious circumstances. Through digging and investigating, the Cassandras had discovered that Rainy
had been murdered. Tory was giving a speech today
about her friend, and she felt Rainy's spirit with her
today, as she sometimes did.

"Why am I not surprised to see you here, Patton?"

Tory glanced over her shoulder to find Shannon
Conner standing a few feet behind her.

"Maybe because I'm giving a speech today?"
Tory wasn't sure what Shannon was getting at. Tory
belonged here. Shannon was the one who'd been
kicked out.

"How is it you always seem to come up golden?"
Shannon asked, but for once there was no malice in
the other woman's voice, only curiosity.

Tory was sure that Shannon didn't want to hear
that Tory had always been careful of the choices she
made. Unlike Shannon, who always seemed to be
looking for shortcuts. To be honest, every situation
Tory found herself in usually worked out the way she
wanted, but she did exert herself to get those results.
Tory shrugged. "Did you uncover anything else
about Andrea and the other hostages?"

"Very little. The trail was cold in Berzhaan, and
once the American group took responsibility, my
network thought I should come back here. My
sources in Suwan indicated that they thought the

hostages had been moved a few days after they were taken."

"The fingertip was mailed from a U.S. post office," Tory said, for some reason sharing with Shannon what she'd learned last night. She'd have to examine that irregular impulse later.

"I heard that at the Pentagon this morning before I flew out here. It was a California postmark. I'm going there after the Athena dedication. You know I wouldn't want to miss this finale to the story I was nominated for an award for, after all."

Tory snorted. Shannon had turned up at the oddest times, with information she shouldn't have had during their investigation into Rainy's death. It turned out that Tory's ex, Perry, had fed Shannon some of her scoops, but the Cassandras still wondered if she'd had another source.

"I'm following some leads as well."

More people were arriving. The school grounds were dotted with families. Tory's parents had been invited, but were unable to make it because of a staff shortage on their ranch.

"I saw your interview with the military protest mom," Shannon said.

"Yeah?"

"It was okay. You always did have a knack for doing a sappy interview."

Shannon could be so nasty when she wanted to be. Tory started to retaliate, but remembered one of her mom's favorite sayings…no one looks good covered in mud.

"Well, Janice Petri has reason to be emotional about her cause. The woman lost her son."

"I'm not criticizing. I just would have handled the interview differently."

"That's what makes each of us unique."

Tory spotted Alex coming toward her and gave Shannon a quick smile. "I'll see you later. I need to talk to Alex before my speech."

She walked away from Shannon and gave Alex a quick hug. "You just saved me from seriously hurting Shannon."

"What did she do this time?" Alex asked, slipping her arm through Tory's.

Tory knew she was going to sound childish, there was no way around it. But Shannon always made her feel as if they were both fourteen again and adversaries. "She called me sappy."

Alex laughed at her. "I can't believe you still let her get to you."

Tory raised both eyebrows at her friend. "This is my career we are discussing. Not petty rivalries."

"Let me remind you, you've won more industry

awards than any of your peers. I think you know you're not sappy."

"Maybe." Tory smiled. "So, who else is here?"

"Sam made it, and I'm sure Kayla's here. Darcy and Josie couldn't come—Darcy's on a trip with Charlie and Jack, and Josie's on some hush-hush Air Force assignment." Alex named the two final members of the Cassandras. "But Kayla told me Rainy's daughter Lynn should be here. She moved to Phoenix and has come by the school a few times."

During their investigation of Rainy's murder, the Cassandras had discovered that Rainy had three daughters she'd never known about, due to a diabolical plan in which her eggs had been mined and stolen by a covert laboratory. In a wild twist, it had turned out that the man Tory and Ben had rescued from Puerto Isla, Tom King, was Lynn and her sisters' biological father. Tory remembered hearing that Lynn had decided to relocate to Phoenix to learn more about her mother. She hoped the young woman was doing as well and looked forward to visiting with her.

She brought up another subject that was on all of their minds. "By the way, I've been so busy concentrating on Andrea I haven't had time to research the Arachne possibility. But I'll get started on it as soon as I return home."

"Me, too." Alex glanced at her watch. "Isn't it almost time for us to be heading over to the assembly?"

The two woman walked together across the campus, reminiscing. The beautiful school grounds soothed Tory's irritation. The school had been built around an old health spa—well, a drying-out facility for rich folks—and the buildings and sweeping lawns were lovely. In the distance Tory could see athletic fields and the stables and riding rings. And beyond, the majestic White Tank Mountains.

As they got closer to the front of the new science wing, where a stage, a podium and perhaps two hundred chairs were set up on the lawn, Tory saw Andrea Jancey's mother and younger sister in the crowd.

"Why is that woman staring at you?" Alex asked, tipping her head toward them.

"That's Andrea Jancey's family. I told her mother I'd give her an update on my investigation today. The Pentagon representative that she's been speaking to has been close-lipped."

"They have to be." Alex glanced at them again, probably trying not to be obvious. "I've never met Mrs. Jancey before. Does the younger girl go to Athena?"

"No. Do you want me to introduce you?" Tory asked.

"Yes, please."

Tory and Alex made their way through the crowd to the Janceys. "Hi, Mrs. Jancey. Hello, Megan. This is Alex Forsythe. She's also a friend of Andrea's from school."

Alex took Mrs. Jancey's hand and then gave the woman a quick hug. "Athena Academy teaches all of us the skills we need to survive. I'm confident you'll see your daughter again."

Mrs. Jancey nodded. "I am, too. Tory, have you discovered anything else about Andrea?"

"Just that we think the hostages are in the U.S. somewhere. And I'm interviewing a man who may have ties to the organization that has claimed responsibility. I'm not going to give up until Andrea is home."

Mrs. Jancey thanked both of them before she and her daughter took their seats.

"There's Kayla!" Alex called out and waved. "And Jazz!"

Tory smiled and also waved to Kayla Ryan and her Athena Academy student daughter. Kayla was now a police lieutenant in Athens, the nearby town. She had her finger on the pulse of all the academy goings-on.

Tory and Alex moved toward the stage. Athena principal Christine Evans gave them warm hugs, and Alex took a seat in the front row. Tory took her place on the platform and reviewed her speech in her head.

"Are you ready for this?" Christine asked.

"Yes."

"You look cool as can be. I know you'll do Rainy proud."

Christine smiled, then brushed efficient hands through her short gray hair and stood up to introduce Troy.

Tory was glad the ceremony was in the middle of the afternoon and not the morning. She felt good, not at all tired or nauseous. For once she felt as if she had the pregnancy under control.

As she spoke her mind wasn't just on Rainy and Athena Academy. It was on the future. As she stared out at the current students and their families. And she read in their eyes the same passion and determination that she'd had herself when she'd first come to the prestigious school. A passion Rainy had embodied. And her professional voice broke just a little, as she honored her late friend and dedicated the school's new wing to the woman to whom all the Cassandras owed a part of whom they'd become.

Tory left Sam, Alex, Lynn and Kayla at the reception to step outside and return a call to Ben. Today had made her think about her own child's future. If she had a daughter, would that child want to go to Athena? It was a family tradition of sorts. Ben's grandfather had been one of the people who'd founded the Academy. Of course, admission was strictly invite only and based on ability.

Ben had been in meetings for the last few days, with his commanding officer and other higher-ups in the military, working on strategy and analyzing information that they'd received.

Jay had narrowed down two areas from the film he'd edited as potential locations for the hostages, and Tory wanted to see if either of them matched what Ben had heard.

She also had to go over her notes for her interview with Larry Maxwell in the morning, and she was still tired. All the pregnancy books she'd read said fatigue was to be expected. Still, Tory was used to operating on very little sleep. Having to actually get a solid eight hours was hard.

She rubbed the back of her neck. She'd focused on the details of Andrea and the other hostages every time she thought of Ben, because she really didn't want to have to think about the fact that he'd asked her to marry him. She wanted to say yes. She loved the man and needed him in a way that, frankly, scared her. And that need was the reason she had asked for time.

"Patton, got a second?"

Tory glanced over her shoulder at Shannon Conner. More than anything, she wanted to finish up her business here and get back to her computer so she could see the images Jay had sent and try to figure out her next move. "Not really, Shannon."

"I think I have some information you could use on that story you're working on."

Tory couldn't ignore one shred of information where Andrea and the hostages were concerned. But why would Shannon willingly share information? The other reporter was always trying to out-scoop her. "I'm listening."

"Come over here, I don't want us to be seen together." Shannon gestured for Tory to join her in the shadows around the corner from the entryway to the reception.

Tory rolled her eyes. "I doubt anyone is going to think we're forming a deep friendship if we're seen talking to each other."

"I'm not concerned about that."

Shannon took her arm and tugged Tory deeper into the shadows. She glanced around once more and then leaned closer to Tory. "I heard you and Alex talking about Arachne before."

For Pete's sake. Shannon needed to stop eavesdropping. "What about it?"

"I had no idea either of you was involved—"

A group of people exited the building before Shannon could say more. None of them glanced to the side as they walked toward the parking lot.

"I'm not involved with Arachne. Can you tell me more about it?"

Tory saw a brief flash of fear in Shannon's eyes. "No. Forget I mentioned it."

Shannon walked away, and Tory stood in the shadows watching her go. What the hell was that all about? She'd tell the others inside. Maybe one of them would be able to make this piece of the puzzle fit.

She dialed Ben's number and waited for him to answer. "Forsythe."

"It's Tory."

"Hey, babe. How was the speech?"

"Good. Kayla, Sam and Rainy's daughter Lynn were there with Alex and me. I feel like Rainy was with us today."

"I bet she was. I can't talk for long, I'm en route to Phoenix. I'll see you soon."

"Where?" Tory asked.

"In your room," he said, his voice dropping lower.

"At the hotel? Alex and I have a connecting suite so she'll probably be with me."

"I'll be late, babe, so you should be sleeping."

"Why should I be sleeping?" she asked. "How late are you going to be?"

"Midnight."

"I think I'll be awake. I never get to bed before two."

"Still?"

"What do you mean, *still?*"

"Just that I've been doing some reading. Women in your…"

It didn't take her any time to figure out where this was going. Did he honestly think that just because she was pregnant she'd forgotten how to take care of herself?

"If you say *condition* I'm going to brain you the next time I see you."

"What word would you suggest? You know I'm with my men. I saw something about physical activity like assaulting me should be kept to a minimum." Laughter was apparent in his voice.

"Bennington Forsythe, are you trying to make me angry?"

"No, just trying to show you that I can be a part of this."

She heard the sincerity in his words. Did he think that was why she hadn't said yes when he'd asked her to marry him? Didn't he realize that his skills as a partner were never in doubt? She took a deep breath.

"I know you can. It's me that I'm worried about, not you. You Forsythes can handle anything the world throws at you."

"So can you, Patton."

"What can I say, that's the way I'm made."

"You don't have to sound defensive. That's one of the traits I admire most about you."

"What else do you admire?" she asked, teasing him because she wanted for just one moment to have something normal between them. Not the tension that had been there since she'd gone to Berzhaan.

"I'll tell you in detail when I get to your room."

"Promise?"

"Damn straight. If you're asleep, I'll wake you up."

"Is your hearing going?"

"No, I'm trying to get you to do what I want without actually giving you an order."

"I'm not one of your men, Ben."

"I know that."

"Good. I have some information on the hostages."

"So do I. We'll talk later."

He disconnected the call and Tory leaned back against the building. The light stone felt cool even in the blazing heat of the late afternoon sunshine.

So much of who she was stemmed from this

place. Even her career had come from what she'd
learned at Athena. She'd always been a people
person, but she also loved unraveling puzzles. Being
a journalist had seemed a natural extension of those
two things.

She eased her way out of the shadows and went
inside to find her friends.

The LASER team was split in two tonight. Half
of them were establishing a central base while the
other half spread out, trying to find more information on Freedom Now. They'd traced two members
to this area of the country and Georgie and L.J. were
hitting the bars in the Phoenix area to search for
more information.

Ben had to be back at their command center at
6:00 a.m. so he had roughly five hours alone with
Tory. O'Neill had secured a key card for Ben to use
to enter Tory's room.

He let himself into her room and found the lights
on. Tory leaned back against the headboard, pillows
piled behind her back and her laptop balanced on her
thighs.

Her eyes were closed, her chest rising and
falling in the pattern of deep sleep. He wanted to
strip down and join her in bed. But there was too
much unsettled between the two of them. He

wasn't making love to her again until she agreed to be his wife.

He glanced at his watch; he was about five minutes early. He checked the door leading to the adjoining room and flipped the lock closed. He didn't want Alex walking in on him and Tory during the night.

He lifted Tory's laptop from her and placed it on the desk. Tory's PDA started beeping and she opened her eyes, reaching over to shut off the alarm. *That little stinker.*

"Busted," he said.

She flushed as she met his eyes across the room. She patted down her hair and sat up straighter against the pillows. Her eyes were sleepy and he wanted nothing more than to just hold her. But he didn't want her to realize how much he needed her. How much he just plain wanted her in his arms, every second of every day.

"When did you get here?"

"In the middle of your nap," he said, sitting down to face her on the bed, taking her hand in his and tracing a pattern on the back.

"So I was sleeping. What of it?" She shrugged.

She had that stubborn look he knew so well. He shook his head. He'd never understand her if they lived a hundred years together.

"I'm glad. I think you're working too hard."

"But I'm doing the same amount of work I usually do," she said. "I can't believe pregnancy is taking such a toll on me. I can't even feel the baby yet."

"What else are you dealing with?" he asked. He'd never been around a pregnant woman before. According to Velosi, pregnant women were hormonal and emotional, going from sweet Madonnas to shrews in the blink of an eye.

"Morning sickness. I'm never sick. It makes me so…"

"What?"

"I don't know. Disgusted. I'm not used to my body being out of control."

"Is there anything I can do?"

She smiled up at him with such affection and tenderness in her face that his breath caught. "No. Thank you."

"What were you working on?" he asked, wanting to get their business out of the way so he could hold her and find some peace for just a few hours.

"The hostages—I've been reviewing the images Jay sent. He spliced the tape that the terrorists sent with stock footage of different barren landscapes. He's really a genius with film."

Ben bit back the jealousy he felt at hearing the

admiration in Tory's voice for another man. "I'm sure he's an editing god."

"I wouldn't go that far," she said, glancing up at him from under her eyelashes. He saw the speculation in her eyes.

"Did he find anything from comparing images?" he asked, reminding himself that she was carrying his child.

"He thinks they're being held in the southwest United States—a desert environment for sure. He's narrowed it to two areas—one here in Arizona, about fifty miles from Phoenix, and a remote area near Palm Springs."

"We're focusing our search in this area of the country as well. Don't bother going to California. That's already been eliminated as a possibility."

"Thanks. I wasn't looking forward to spending any more time on a plane until I go home."

"Flying not agreeing with you?" he asked. He shifted around on the bed until she was cradled against his side. He tipped her head back and claimed the kiss he'd been wanting since he entered the room.

"We had some turbulence on the flight in. I almost had to use the barf bag and Alex would have started asking questions I'm not ready to answer yet."

"Have you told anyone about the baby?"

"Only you."

"We can't tell your parents until you agree to marry me."

"Why not?"

"Because they don't like me."

"They don't understand why you're always being photographed with other women."

"Is that why you won't marry me?"

"I don't want to talk about that. I trust you, Ben."

"Good. I'm going to talk to my CO when we have the hostages back about taking a desk job."

She frowned at him. "You'd never be happy behind a desk."

"I'm not happy being away from you, either."

"Really?"

He didn't answer that. "What other leads are you following?"

"I have an e-mail in to Diana Lockworth. She's a fellow Athena grad and *really* close to the President, so she should have a great insider's perspective on the mood in Washington. I'm waiting to hear back from her. I also e-mailed Tom King about Freedom Now, but he didn't have any other information."

"O'Neill, our computer guy, has been working on hacking into Freedom Now's Web site. He's found several messages from the organization that mention this part of the country. He's still deciphering the rest of the messages."

"I'm interviewing Larry Maxwell tomorrow. I think he's a member of the group. I haven't been able to confirm it yet. One of our researchers found some Internet chat sites where he'd participated and the group's name came up, but nothing substantial."

"I'll have O'Neill run his name. If he is a part of this group…"

"What? Don't even say you don't want me to interview him."

"Of course, I'm going to say that. It would prove that he's not above taking members of the media for his cause."

"We don't know that he has anything to do with this."

"You're right. I just don't want you in danger."

"I'm not. I'm very competent at what I do, Ben."

"Remember Suwan?"

"That was random. I could have been anyone. And they went after you, too."

"It doesn't change the fact that you could have been killed," he said. He pulled her into his arms. He still had nightmares about that, probably would until the day he died. What kind of man let his woman step into that type of situation?

Tory's arms snaked around his waist and she

rested her head right over his heart. "You could have died, too."

They held each other on the bed for a long time, neither one saying anything else, but both knowing that their lives needed to change if they were going to be parents to the child Tory carried in her womb.

Chapter 12

Tory wanted to drift to sleep in Ben's arms. It would give her a safe way to escape from having to talk to him about the subject they'd both danced around. She couldn't believe a man as straightforward and determined as Ben was not demanding an answer to his proposal.

When he'd mentioned taking a desk job, she'd known that things between them were stronger than she'd wanted to admit. Because then she'd have to really start making changes to her life. Until she'd gotten pregnant she hadn't realized how selfish she could be. She didn't want to mean so much to Ben that he would sacrifice the career he loved for her.

It was complicated, she thought. But then, self-evaluation was. But she knew at the heart of the matter was the fact that she didn't know if she'd be able to make the sacrifices Ben made worthwhile. Was she enough to keep him happy and content for the rest of their lives?

What if he grew to resent her? She would hate to see that charming rogue with whom she'd fallen in love change to a man worn down by a mundane career.

She shifted around until she could look up at Ben, unsure what to say to him. How could they bridge the gap in what they both wanted from life and what they both would have to be for their child?

"What?"

"Nothing," she said, taking the coward's way out and bowing her head. His heart beat steadily under her cheek and she closed her eyes, surrounding herself with his warmth, his scent. It was soothing in a way she couldn't explain even to herself.

"I know you were thinking about something," he said, rubbing his chin against her head.

"How do you know that?" she asked, stalling. Her normally quick mind wasn't up to playing games like she usually did.

"Tory Patton, your mind is always full of something," he said, smoothing his hands down her back and caressing her backside.

She wiggled around until she rested on top of him, her hands on his chest and her chin on her hands. She looked up at him and saw that familiar, playful look in his eyes. "That's very true."

"So?" he asked.

For a minute she was tempted to admit the truth—that she was thinking about them and their relationship. But she had no answers to the questions between them. Not yet, and she needed more time to figure out the future for herself, before she could talk about it with Ben.

"I was thinking about my interview for tomorrow."

"Anything I can help with? Is Shawna going with you?"

"She's driving out with the cameraman."

"Good, maybe she can keep you from getting into trouble."

She mock-punched his jaw. "Maxwell wouldn't come to D.C. for an interview with me. I'm going to his ranch. Do you think that's significant?"

Ben rubbed his hands up and down her back, pulling her more snuggly against his body.

"He might have thought it would discourage you from interviewing him."

"He doesn't know me very well."

"No, he doesn't. Let me contact O'Neill and I'll see what we can find out about him. I don't want you walking into a dangerous situation."

"Didn't we already have this conversation?" she asked.

He rolled them over so that she was pinned beneath his body. "I thought it was worth repeating. You don't always listen well."

She kissed him hard on the lips and slid her hands down his back to pinch his butt. "Stop being so bossy."

"You know you love it," he said, levering himself up and off of her. He sat up on the bed and grabbed his cell phone from the nightstand, then moved away to make his call. She watched him. His body was lean and hard. He worked out hard to keep himself in top shape. He was able to handle every situation he was put into because he'd made himself into a weapon. His career wasn't just a job, it was his life.

She shut down her computer and quietly changed into her pajamas while Ben was on the phone. He made two calls after the one to O'Neill and she made an effort not to listen to his calls. She wasn't going to start prying into his investigation. She respected what he could tell her.

"O'Neill will call when he finds something on

Maxwell. I asked him to put a rush on it. Hopefully he'll get back to me before your interview. I know I'll feel better once I have some background."

"I'm not going alone. The cameraman is Jay Matthews. He's going with me, and so is Shawna. You know someone would have to be crazy to mess with the three of us."

"I know that someone kidnapped a reporter, her cameraman and translator. *Three of them.* I don't think the odds are in your favor."

"I can't not go, Ben. I'm close to something on this story. I know it, and I think you know it, too."

"I'm not saying to cancel it, just give me a day or so to get every bit of information I can about this guy."

"I can't postpone it. I have to be back in D.C. at the beginning of the week for my show. We have a panel of experts who are going to talk about the terrorists' demands and the U.S. reaction to them from political and personal standpoints."

"Dammit. I don't like it."

"Trust me. It's an interview—what could go wrong?"

"In theory nothing, but something about this entire setup makes me leery."

"Could it be because I'm pregnant?"

He rubbed the back of his neck. "Yeah, it could

be. I want to wrap you in cotton and put you some-place safe."

"I wouldn't let you."

"Hell, I know that. But it doesn't change the way I feel."

Tory didn't know what to say. This was precisely what made her so reluctant to have Ben give up the job he loved for a desk job. She couldn't be the woman he wanted her to be. Even if she were willing to change, neither of them would be happy.

"Are we talking all night, or getting some sleep?" she asked. "I hate to admit it, but you were right. I do need more sleep than I used to."

"Of course I'm right."

"Don't be arrogant. How would you know anything about pregnant women?"

"I told you, I picked up a book."

"I can't imagine you reading a book on pregnancy. What did your men say?"

"Nothing. I hid it beneath the dust cover of a military thriller."

"Ah, how exciting to get a peek into the mind of a covert operative," she said.

Ben growled at her, grabbing her around the waist and bringing them both down on the bed. He cuddled closer to her.

"Are we sleeping on top of the covers?"

"I can't stay here tonight. I have to get back to the men. They may have found a man who knows something about the Freedom Now group. We're going to question him."

She nodded. He pulled her into his arms for a fierce hug before he got up, crossed the room and walked out the door. Be safe, she thought, but didn't call out to him. Instead she locked the dead bolt on the hotel door and slipped into bed, tucking the pillow Ben had lain on against her stomach.

"Russ, you got a minute?"

"Yes." Russ was happy to step outside of the hunting cabin away from the hostages for a few minutes. It had been almost three days since they'd sent the fingertip, and they had received almost no response from the military.

Russ was almost sick thinking about what they had to do next. They'd decided on this course of action so that there would be no more death and killing. And now they were going to have to kill one of the hostages to get the attention of President Monihan.

"What's up?"

"That reporter who called for an interview is coming to my ranch."

"When?"

"Tomorrow. I put her off until the afternoon. I didn't know what else to do."

Russ wasn't sure, either. But he didn't let it show. Another reporter. But this one they could use. "Where'd she get your name?"

"From Janice Petri, I think."

Janice was Rodney's ex-wife and a pain in everyone's ass. It could have been spite or just plain meanness on Janice's part to sic the reporter on them.

"What'd she say she wanted to talk to you about?"

"Garret, I think, and the current situation. She already interviewed Janice, so I guess she wants to know more about why we started the organization."

"What are you going to tell her?"

"I have no idea. That's why I wanted to talk to you. I figured I'd just say I was pissed when the officers came to tell me about Garret."

But Larry hadn't been pissed, he'd been shattered. The same as Russ had been when he'd heard about Tommy. The same as all the parents were when they got the news that one of their own children was dead.

Russ turned his back on Larry and looked out at the horizon. What were they going to do? An interview with Larry could help them convince Congress to pressure the president to pull out.

"I think you should forget anger and tell her the truth. Let her see the grief you still feel."

"I don't know, Russ. Once I start thinking about Garret...I don't always keep it together."

Russ put his hand on his friend's shoulder. "I'll go with you. If things get too bad I'll interrupt everything. I was going to Phoenix today anyway, to meet that medic."

"What time is your appointment?"

"Five. What time is your interview?"

"Two-thirty."

"Perfect. We can handle them both."

Rodney and Jake were in D.C., and two other men from Russ's inner group were coming in to guard the hostages today. Russ had devised a schedule that would keep the men fresh and alert. He didn't want to chance any screwups.

The interview with Larry was unexpected, but Russ was confident they could handle one little television reporter. He didn't want another hostage.

"If she asks me about Freedom Now, what should I do? I thought I'd pretend not to have heard of the group."

"You can't. The demands of the group have been all over the media. You'd sound like an idiot. Just say that you hadn't heard of the group until they showed up on the news."

"You think that'll work?" Larry asked. "It's that Tory Patton. Alice watches her show all the time.

She's a real bulldog, never stopping until she gets to the bottom of the story."

Russ really had no idea what would work. Reactions were always hard to predict, but Russ did know that Larry was good at playing down his wealth and acting like a good old boy rancher who'd lost his son. He was good with people, and Russ thought that his friend wouldn't have much trouble charming the lady reporter.

He also knew that if Larry believed he could pull off the interview, he had a better chance of actually doing it.

"Yes. Just remember to look her in the eye the whole time. Don't do anything to let her know you're lying to her."

Larry had been a POW, so Russ wasn't worried about the reporter getting any secrets out of him. If the Vietcong couldn't get information from him, she wouldn't, either.

No names were listed anywhere on the Freedom Now Web site or on the letter they'd sent to the Joint Chiefs, so Larry couldn't be linked to the group. In fact, no one could. They had a secure server and all of them used code names that only someone familiar with the military might be able to decipher.

"What's our next move going to be?" Larry asked. "I don't want to send another fingertip to them."

"We're going to have to step up the pressure. Rodney is going to feel out his contacts and see if they're close to pulling out. If not, then we'll have to kill one of the hostages."

Larry didn't say anything else and Russ was glad for that. He didn't want to have to think about the hostages or their families. Russ never forgot that he was causing grief to the families of the young people they'd taken. It didn't deter him from his mission.

Russ didn't like to think about killing. They'd started this entire mission to stop the needless deaths. But sometimes violence was the only way to get attention. And he wasn't about to back down from what they'd sworn to do—to keep any other parents from getting a message from the State Department.

Tory met Jay and Shawna in the lobby of the hotel around noon. She'd compiled a nice file of research on Larry Maxwell. From all accounts, he was a gregarious man who was well-liked by everyone. The small ranching community he lived in on the outskirts of Phoenix had once elected him mayor. He lived with his wife on the ranch and they had two children still living. Both of those children were grown and had families of their own.

"Do you have your questions ready for Maxwell?"

Shawna asked as they drove through traffic in Phoenix.

"I've got a lot of questions. I'll use different ones, depending on his answers."

"I think you should definitely hit on the incident with the Marines who brought the news of his son's death."

"I will. That seems to be what led to the creation of Janice Petri's group. I'm going to float Freedom Now out there and see how he reacts."

"Sounds good. Jay, I want you to shoot some cutaways of the surrounding area, see if it matches what we found in the hostage tape."

"Sure thing," Jay said. "Are we going to be live?"

"Not with Maxwell, but Tory, how do you feel about doing something live from the desert for tonight's show? Then we can catch a late flight back to D.C."

"That works for me. Should we mention that our investigation has led us to the desert area?" Tory asked, not sure if it was wise to tip their hand to Freedom Now.

"What do you think?"

"I'm still not sure. Let's see what we get from Maxwell and then decide. I don't want to force them to do anything drastic."

"It won't be us that forces them to do something,

it'll be the government. What was the deadline for some sort of action?"

"Midnight tonight," Tory said, without consulting her notes. She knew that time was running out. The terrorists had to feel the pressure, too. The government wouldn't respond to their anonymous letters and the media hadn't been approached to air any sort of rebuttal from the leaders of Freedom Now.

Tory made more notes on a small pad while they drove through the city, each of them quiet and preparing for the upcoming taping. Tory's mind turned from Larry Maxwell to Ben. She hated that things between them were still so unresolved.

Deliberately, she forced herself to stop dwelling on him and turned her thoughts back to the interview. In her mind she had an image of the fifty-eight-year-old man. He was a successful rancher, a decorated veteran who'd been a POW. The words came in her mind how she would describe him, how she would set up her interview with him for her audience.

As they neared the small town of Palmer Junction, Tory sat up. A plaque under the population sign honored Larry Maxwell and his son Garret for their sacrifice.

"Pull over here, Jay. I want to get some tape of that sign. Maybe I can do a little intro from here."

"Good thinking, Tory."

Tory smiled at Shawna. "I'm going to touch up my makeup while you guys scout for the best location to shoot from."

"Do we have anything on Palmer Junction? Something like an all-American town where American pride and patriotism run high…what do you think, Shawna?"

"Call research and have them pull what they can on the town. We'll go with what you have for now and then edit later if need be."

Tory called research and left a message for Cathy, then finished applying the heavy layer of makeup she needed for on-camera filming. She wore jeans and a silk shirt with a light summer blazer. It was hot today, nearing almost 100 degrees.

She checked her hair in the mirror and then emerged from the van. "I'm going to stand still. Just get me from the waist up so I don't have to change out of my jeans until we get to Maxwell's ranch."

"No problem, Tory."

Only a few vehicles passed them while they were filming, then they returned to their news van and arrived at the Maxwell ranch in less than fifteen minutes.

They stopped under a huge wrought-iron arch that marked the entrance to the sprawling Maxwell ranch. Tory again got out of the van to shoot some cutaways and to talk about the family she was there to interview. They'd cut these shots with a voice-over in editing to round out the interview.

Tory changed into a skirt that matched her suit jacket in the back of the van before they drove down the mile-long driveway to the house, a two-story adobe. Cacti grew in a flowerbed in front and boxes with bring colored annuals, parched from the heat of the day, decorated the windows. Two wooden rockers sat on either side of the door.

Jay walked around outside the house, shooting it from different angles while Shawna and Tory talked to Alice and Larry Maxwell. They decided to tape the interview in the couple's den. One wall was filled with all the honors that Larry had received. There was an eight-by-ten photo of Garret Maxwell in his Marine Corps uniform as well.

They rearranged the furniture so that Larry was seated under the photo of his deceased son and the pictures of other two kids, Marcia and Baker. Baker, Larry informed them, was in the Coast Guard and Marcia was a stay-at-home mom.

The house was filled with crafts that the Maxwells' children and grandchildren had made. More photos lined the hallways, and Alice spoke lovingly of their life together, and about the monthly trips she and Larry took to visit their grandchildren.

While looking at the pictures Tory felt the story snap into place. This was a man who put family before everything else—and would do whatever he had to do to defend them.

Chapter 13

O'Neill broke the code used to encrypt Freedom Now's back-end Web site. No names were listed, only codenames, but there was information. The group had been soliciting someone with medical training for a special assignment through their newsgroup.

"Do you think this is for the guy whose fingertip they chopped off?" O'Neill asked, handing Ben a piece of paper from the compact printer.

Ben scanned the message, which was pretty brief. "Probably. Is it possible for us to intercept?"

O'Neill went back to his computer. "Not sure yet. I need to find out who this guy is."

"You haven't yet?" Ben asked. O'Neill had been working at his computer for almost twenty-four hours. The LASER team all felt the pressure to get to Paul Manning and the other hostages before it was too late.

O'Neill shrugged at him. "I'm not a miracle worker. I should have at least an e-mail for the guy they contacted in the next few minutes."

Ben left O'Neill at the computer and moved through the small house they were renting to find Velosi. Lewis was sprawled in front of a television set playing *Badge of Courage* on a PSP 2 game console. Ben sat down next to him on the couch. "You might be going undercover."

"As what? I'm not really good at being a playboy like you." Velosi never looked up from his game. Lewis was extremely good at multitasking, as were all of his men.

"Ha. You just be yourself. O'Neill thinks that Freedom Now is looking for someone with medical training who won't ask too many questions."

"Okay, when?" Velosi asked.

"Sometime today or tomorrow. O'Neill should have a timeline for us soon. Are we any closer to the implant GPS chip?"

Since Manning's kidnapping, the LASER team had been trying to participate in a new program the military had where they implanted GPS homing beacons under the skin of all personnel. Ben wasn't too sure he wanted the government to always know where he was, but if their team had been implanted, finding Manning would have been infinitely easier.

Velosi paused the action on the television. The older man gave him a shrewd look. "You want me to come up with something unauthorized?"

"Can you?"

"Maybe. It's not really my area of expertise. I'll have to look at the GPS beacon we have in one of the cell phones."

"Do it. I'm not losing another man to this group."

Ben watched the other man's reaction, for the first time understanding him a little better. Understanding what Velosi had to lose if a mission got screwed up. The wife and child that Velosi had waiting for him were suddenly real to Ben. And the man with whom he'd had nothing in common, other than fighting in this unit, was suddenly more of a comrade.

"The timetable is tight—we're not sure we have even a couple of hours."

"Damn. There's no way I can get an implant that quickly. I could swallow a GPS beacon, but it's going to pass in twenty-four hours or so."

That might not be a bad thing, since Ben planned on moving quickly. But so far they weren't sure where in the desert the hostages were being held and it could take time to get to Velosi. He wasn't about to leave another one of his men vulnerable. "Give me a couple of options, Velosi."

"Will do," Velosi said, leaving the couch and going into the bedroom where he'd been bunking.

Ben rubbed his face with both hands. His mind spun with endless possibilities and all of them came back to the one fact that time was running out, and they needed to take action now.

Georgie and Potchicki both sat in another corner of the room, going over their weapons, as usual. Georgie looked up. "Are you going to want us to provide cover?"

"Yes. We need more intel before I can give you details. Get on your desert cammies and meet me in the kitchen in fifteen."

Ben strode from the living room back to the small den, almost running over O'Neill, who was coming out of the room. "What did you find?"

"They're meeting the guy tonight. Bill Jones. He's driving in from Palm Springs. I think we can intercept if we leave now."

"What kind of car does he drive?"

"A big old Escalade with OnStar."

"Do you have his current location?" Ben asked. O'Neill had hacked into the OnStar system before. The automotive companies used the system to unlock doors for its consumers, call 911 after accidents and provide all manner of information to drivers. But the government and Ben's team used the system when they needed to find an exact GPS location of a vehicle.

"He's headed our way. I think we can apprehend him, here," O'Neill said, handing a map to Ben.

"How sure are you that this is our man?"

"Ninety percent. There's been a lot of activity around trying to find someone with medical experience on the newsgroup. They've been quiet prior to that, and once this guy spoke up, the group went almost silent again."

Ben didn't want them going off in a wrong direction. But the timing was fast, so if they nabbed the wrong guy, they could quickly change directions if they needed to.

"Gather our men and meet at the Hummer."

O'Neill left and Ben pulled out his Blackberry and sent a quick message to his CO, informing him that they had some new intel and were moving on it.

Ben met outside. He knew they were anxious to find their friend.

Moving quickly and making decisions on the run was what they were used to. And they all wanted to get Manning back. After their briefing at the Pentagon, they all knew that time was running out.

Freedom Now would be feeling the pressure to act once again, because the U.S. government was not negotiating with terrorists and they'd made a statement to that affect in this morning's papers.

"Let's move out. O'Neill has a lock on the guy Freedom Now is bringing in. We're going to try to make a switch before he gets to his meeting place."

"We're ready to roll."

Less than ten minutes later, Ben was driving the Hummer with O'Neill riding shotgun. Salvo, Georgie, Potchicki and Velosi were all seated in the back.

"O'Neill, bring everyone up to date." Ben kept his eyes on the road and focused on intercepting Bill Jones. They found a stretch of a two-lane highway on Jones's route that was practically deserted and set up their ambush. Georgie and Potchicki went to ground nearby to provide cover in case Jones wasn't amenable to cooperating with them.

Velosi swallowed the GPS beacon and the other men waited for the Escalade to come into their sights. A certain calm fell over the group as they prepared for what they did best—action.

The interview was going smoothly. Larry was a gracious interviewee who seemed open and honest about his experiences. Jay had set up for a wide shot that would include both her and Larry Maxwell.

They were sitting on a love seat facing each other at a 45-degree angle. It was an intimate setting and Tory realized she preferred the distance her usual separate chairs stage setup gave her.

She'd asked Larry to describe what had happened when he got the news that his son was dead.

"When I got the word about Garret, I felt like my entire life had collapsed. In one second I went from having it all to…having nothing."

He rubbed a hand over his face and glanced away from the camera. Tory put her hand on his arm, waiting for him to compose himself.

"Did you consider your other children?"

"In that moment, I didn't think of anything except the hole left in our lives by Garret's death. My wife was screaming…my God, do you know what that does to a man?"

Tory didn't know from first-hand experience, but she'd witnessed that kind of grief before. And for a moment, she thought of Ben and how she'd felt when Alex had been waiting for her in his D.C. apartment. How the grief and numbness had rushed through her at the thought of him being gone.

She waited for him to compose himself, glancing at her notes before moving on. She didn't want to dwell on the kind of pain that Larry was talking about. Didn't want to think about the fact that Ben placed himself in danger every day to keep his military brothers safe. Didn't want to acknowledge that someday she might be sitting where Larry Maxwell had been when those Marines had come to deliver the news of his son's death.

"What do you say to action groups like Freedom Now, who have taken three Americans hostage?" she asked. "The two men and one woman they've taken have family and friends who are all being placed in the same position you were when you received the news of your son's death."

"Well, those kids are still alive and I pray that the government will do whatever they need to do so that they aren't killed. There's been enough killing and it's time to find a peaceful solution."

"Have you participated in Military Parents In Support of Withdrawal Now?"

"I'm not much of a letter writer, but I have spoken to Senator Bill Fresi about it. Urged him to do what he can to get our troops home where they can be safe. My wife has made some calls to different congressmen."

"You seem much more a man of action," Tory said. "Do you feel like our government under President Monihan has left you with no choices?"

"We always have choices," Larry said. "Sometimes they're hard and sacrifices have to be made, but there are choices."

Tory wasn't sure what he was alluding to. She imagined that men like Ben and her brother Derrick, who was a DEA agent, would understand him.

"What kind of choices?" she asked, forcing her mind back to the interview. This piece cut too close to home for her. She hadn't done a story that had affected her this personally since her brother had been injured asking questions on her behalf almost two years ago.

"Ones that you wouldn't make during peacetime." Larry glanced out the window, away from her and the camera.

Tory knew that there was more here than what Larry was saying—something important that he'd reveal if she just asked the right question. But she didn't know what direction to go in. "You were in Vietnam, weren't you?"

He nodded. "I did two tours there."

Tory leaned forward, bringing Larry's attention back to the room and the camera. The interview would look weird when they edited it, if he were still staring at something outside.

"Did you have to make choices there? Hard choices?" Tory asked.

"In wartime, there's only one decision a warrior makes every day—whether he's going to kill or be killed. The guys I served with are still some of my closest friends even though we don't see each other all that often."

"Who are those men?"

"No one you would have heard of—just average Joes who did their part for patriotism."

"Just like your son," she said. "Did Garret join the military because you had?"

"I couldn't say for sure. We never talked about anything like that, but the men in my family have been Marines for as long as we can remember."

She wondered if that had been part of the rage that Larry had felt. Men in his family had been serving this country for a long time, fighting in wars they may or may not have believed in.

"Do you think the troops in the Middle East are facing the same decision you did when you were in Vietnam…kill or be killed?"

"Yes, ma'am, I do. Except they don't know what their enemy looks like. They can't fight a suicide bomber."

He stopped talking. Tory knew that Garret Maxwell had been killed by a suicide bomber who'd blown up his car in front of a military checkpoint. She didn't want to bring that out in the open now though. She'd do it in a voice-over.

"Our sons and daughters are facing that decision

every day and it's for a cause that no one really understands," Larry added.

Tory knew she had to get the interview back on track. "You're not opposed to military action, are you?"

"Not at all. What I'm opposed to is senseless death," Larry said.

That was a great place to end the interview. Larry had given her a perfect sound bite to use to promote the piece and lead into her story.

"Thank you for your time, Larry."

"Thank you for coming to Arizona to speak to me."

"It was my pleasure."

She signaled to Jay to turn the camera off.

"We're done now. Jay will take off your microphone and battery pack. Do you mind if we walk around your property with you and your wife?"

"Why?"

"So that Jay can shoot some footage of the two of you. We'll cut it together with the interview footage in the final piece."

"I'll go check with Alice. I think she's in the middle of baking bread for the Palmer Junction heritage celebration this Saturday. Her ladies group always has a bake sale."

"Thanks, Larry, for checking with her," Tory said. But something about the way he said that last bit made her suspicious. Larry wasn't the kind of man who'd waffle on something as simple as a few outside shoots.

"While you're checking, is there a bathroom I could use?"

Larry stared at something behind her. His eyes widened and then he looked back at her. Tory glanced over her shoulder but saw nothing, just an empty hallway.

"Second door on the left," he said, gesturing down the empty hall.

Ben rubbed the back of his neck, willing away the niggling tension there. He flagged down Bill Jones's black Escalade. The man they'd been tracking via GPS satellite was in his late forties and wore glasses.

The LASER team was split. Georgie and Potchicki lying in prone position and providing cover from about fifty yards out, Velosi, Salvo and O'Neill hidden in the back of the Hummer. He was connected to his team via wireless microphones and earpieces.

"I've got the target in sight," he told them.

The Escalade pulled up next to Ben's position and Ben was careful to stay clear of Bill Jones so that his snipers would have a clear view of the man if need be.

"What's the problem?" Jones asked, not getting out of his vehicle.

"Battery, I think. Can you give me a jump?"

"Sure thing. Give me a minute to turn around."

The Escalade pulled around and soon was facing hood-to-hood with the Hummer. The man got out of the SUV and Ben waited for him to approach.

"Thanks, man, for stopping. I've been stuck here for a while. I'm Ben, by the way."

"Bill," the other man said, sticking his hand out for Ben to shake. "No problem. I can't drive by and leave someone stranded."

"Why not?"

"I'm an EMT. I think it's in my blood."

"Confirmed that Bill Jones is an EMT," O'Neill said in Ben's ear.

Ben waited, wanting to be as close to one hundred percent sure they had the right guy before he took him into custody and exchanged their man for him.

"Where you from?" Ben asked as he attached the jumper cables to the battery in his Hummer.

"Palm Springs."

"What brings you out this way?" Ben asked.

Bill took the jumper cables from Ben and set them near the engine on his vehicle. "I'm meeting up with some former military buddies."

"Sounds like our man, boss."

"You attach the cables when I get back in my car."

Ben nodded and waited for Bill to start his SUV before attaching the cables to the other engine. He climbed in the Hummer and started the engine.

"I'll apprehend him when he retrieves the jumper cables."

"We'll be ready. But he doesn't match Velosi's coloring at all," O'Neill said.

"I'm aware of that. Depending on how quickly we get information from him, we might have to dye your hair, Velosi."

"I can take care of that," Salvo said. He started digging in his backpack. Ben got out of the Hummer. The engine purred smoothly. He detached the jumper cables from his engine and then from Bill's.

The other man got back out of his vehicle.

"Thanks again for stopping," Ben said, holding his hand out.

The other man took it and Ben used his grip to draw Bill in closer to his body. Rotating Bill's wrist by turning the hand outwards so that the palm was facing upward.

"What the hell are you doing, man?"

"Bill Jones?"

"Yes."

"The United States government needs to ask you a few questions."

Bill brought his right fist up and punched Ben

hard in the face, putting his weight behind his hand and tugging to free himself. Ben shook off the blow, which hurt like a mother, and used his grip on Bill's left wrist to force the man to his knees. Ben grabbed his free hand and quickly bound Bill's wrists with a zip cord.

"Who the hell *are* you?" Bill asked.

"I'll handle the questions. Are you a part of Freedom Now?"

The man flushed, but didn't look away. He said nothing.

O'Neill, Salvo and Velosi climbed from the Hummer and together the men forced Bill into their vehicle.

"Listen, Bill, this can go one of two ways. You can answer our questions and go home relatively quickly or we can arrest you, question you in an interrogation room and toss you in the brig until you're an old man," Ben said.

"I don't know anything about Freedom Now. I'm in a newsgroup with other ex-military men and one guy was asking for someone with medical training to help out in a field exercise. Last I heard, that wasn't against the law."

Ben didn't feel a flicker of guilt. He'd read the e-mail that O'Neill had found from Bill Jones. This man knew perfectly well who he was working with.

"Who is your contact?"

Bill said nothing.

"When are you meeting?"

Again no answer. Salvo pulled his weapon, a Sig-Sauer handgun, and put the barrel to the side of Bill's temple. "Ask him again."

Bill swallowed and a bead of sweat ran down the side of his face.

"Who is your contact?" Ben asked.

"I'm meeting someone with the code name Uncle Sam."

"Where is the meeting going to take place?" Ben asked to confirm what they'd read in the e-mail.

"At the Watering Hole in Phoenix."

O'Neill started punching information into his computer.

"What time?"

"Five-thirty this evening. Now move the gun."

Salvo dropped his weapon. Ben and his men assessed their timetable. "We're going to take you to a safe house for the time being, Bill."

Bill nodded. It was almost three so they had enough time to get back to Phoenix and set Velosi up as Bill Jones.

"Have you met any of the men in person before?"

"No."

"How will they recognize you?"

"I'm to go to the bar and order a Bud in the bottle. Then wait at a table in the dart room, for my contact."

"What's the word exchange you're using for identifying each other?"

Bill hesitated. Salvo raised his weapon again.

"My contact will say, 'Hot enough for you?' And I'm to respond, 'Yes, but at least it's a dry heat.'"

"Thanks for your cooperation, Bill."

The other man didn't say anything. Ben called in Georgie and Potchicki. Salvo joined them in Bill's Escalade and they all headed back toward Phoenix.

"Did they tell you what kind of injury to expect?" Ben continued to question Bill.

"Not really. They mentioned gangrene and tetanus plus dehydration."

Ben's gut tightened, knowing how dangerous those conditions were for anyone. It had been over a week since the hostages had been taken, and it sounded like time was running out.

Chapter 14

Russ waited until the news team left Larry's house before coming out of his hiding place in the upstairs bedroom. He'd had a moment of panic when he'd almost run into the reporter in the hallway, but then the group had gone outside and left without incident.

Alice had gone into town to meet with a planning committee for the heritage festival, so Larry and he were alone. They had a little over two hours before they were to meet up with Bill Jones.

"I think the interview went well," Larry said, handing him a bottle of beer as they both gathered food and supplies to return to the hunting cabin.

"Let's move out. I want to get a feel for the Watering Hole before we're supposed to meet this Jones guy." Russ didn't like to be away from the hostages for this long. He trusted the men he'd recruited to a certain extent but he liked to stay on top of every detail.

Larry paused in the hallway by the picture of Garret. Next to it was a picture of Tommy and Garret when they'd both enlisted. Russ and Larry had gone with the boys to the recruiting office. The picture was a painful reminder of the joy and pride that Russ had felt on that day.

"I can round up some local boys to meet us there if you want more cover."

Russ glanced away from his young son's face and back at the weathered lines on his friend's. "No. The fewer people who see Jones with us, the better."

"We're not planning to kill him, are we?" Larry asked, pausing again in the hallway. The summer afternoon sun filled the space with bright light and for a minute, Russ wished they could go back to a simpler time when the two of them could have been meeting to go fishing for the weekend. Instead, the world had changed and those simple joys no longer brought him the peace they once had.

His resolution had never wavered and it didn't now, standing in his friend's nice home and talking about death. It seemed his life went in cycles of peace and war. His childhood home had been filled with peace until his mother's death when he was six. Then it had been a combat zone with his old man until he left for 'Nam and four long years of war. Afterward he'd met his wife, Betty, and they'd had eighteen years of peace. Now he was at war again. What was it about him that seemed to be drawn time and again to conflict?

"Russ? Are we going to have to take out Jones?"

Russ didn't answer. Jones was an unknown, and if the man balked at what they'd done so far and the government didn't respond the way they wanted to, then Jones might become a liability. He shrugged. "We'll do whatever we have to. If that means killing this EMT, then so be it."

"What are we going to do with the bodies?" Larry asked.

Russ had already thought about it. They had body bags and pine boxes ready for transport if they were forced to use them. "Send them to Washington, I think that should get their attention. We'll use your plane. Rodney and Jake are already in D.C., setting it up."

Larry nodded. "I wish there were some way to lessen the loss. That reporter asked me about choices and I wanted to tell her that President Monihan has made some terrible ones. Ones that are directly responsible for the pain this country is experiencing right now with the loss of so many young people."

"There is. President Monihan needs to pull the troops out. Public support for his actions is waning."

"What if we kill all three and he still won't give in?"

Russ didn't want to contemplate that happening. He hadn't planned for that contingency. He'd figured a man like President Monihan would buckle as soon as the Americans were taken.

"We need to step up pressure. Have Janice and her group stage a protest outside the White House or at Camp David. Then we need to issue another press release. Do you have contact information for that reporter you just spoke to?"

"Yes, I have her phone numbers," Larry said. He walked into his study and came back out with a piece of paper that had cell and work numbers.

Russ put the paper in his pocket as they left Larry's house. He tossed the keys to his truck to Larry. "You drive. I'm going to make a few calls and see if we can't use the media to make the president move the way we want him to."

"What are you going to say?"

"That the hostages being taken is a direct result of the actions of the U.S. government and their unlawful interference in Middle East. There's no reason for us to be a continued presence in Berzhaan now that the Kemeni rebels aren't a threat."

"A lot of our veterans were interviewed on the Fourth. We can ask them to get back on the air and start spreading the word."

"I want to be careful that whoever goes to the media doesn't have any direct connection with Freedom Now."

Larry entered the highway heading toward Phoenix. "No one is listed on the Web site so we should be good."

"I'm going to check in with Pete and make sure that the public site is still holding." Pete Williams had designed two Web sites for their group and was in charge of making sure that hackers didn't enter the second site where they had encrypted message boards. Someone had been trying to access their records and archives over the past twenty-four hours, and Pete had some kind of high-tech thing to keep the hacker from getting through.

Russ didn't understand computers or technology too well. He knew how to use his PC, but anything too techie he left to Pete. Whoever was probing around their Web site made Russ leery. He knew that time was running out for the hostages. The government was delaying and Russ figured it was either because they didn't think Freedom Now was serious, or they were trying to find Freedom Now. Which meant that he and his men needed to act. The time for waiting was over.

Tory sat alone in the local affiliate station of UBC, reviewing the tape of the interview she'd conducted with Larry Maxwell. Jay had gotten some great shots and she marked the ones she wanted edited together. Jay had stepped out for a cigarette.

She paused on a cutaway shot that Jay had gotten of the hallway wall. The wall had been covered in photos from the chair rail to the ceiling. Some of the photos were clearly professional, while others were framed snapshots. She froze the screen on one that showed Garret Maxwell and another young man with their arms slung around each other's shoulders, standing in front of a strip-mall recruiting office for the Marines.

Who was the other guy? She slowly reran the tape of the hallway and found two other photos on the wall with the same kid. There was one when they were both in their early teens at a hunting cabin. The boys were holding the antlers of a deer. The other one was taken at Carlsbad Cavern.

Tory jotted down the time code of the other pictures, hoping she could find the other boy and maybe interview him. Obviously he was military, and maybe he'd offer a different perspective on Garret Maxwell.

Leaning back in her chair, she patted her stomach, wondering who her child's friends would be. Would her friendships change as her child was born and started making bonds? She'd have to have a long talk with Kayla and Darcy, the two Cassandras who had kids, once this hostage crisis was over.

Not having answers was something she didn't like so she switched gears and glanced through her notes. Where had Garret been recruited? Here in Phoenix.

She did a quick Internet search and hit pay dirt. An article in the *Palmer Junction Gazette* reported on two hometown boys who'd enlisted together— Garret Maxwell and Tom Dorn. The article included the names of the boys' families—including their fathers, who had both been Vietnam war heroes. Larry Maxwell and Russ Dorn.

The next thing she found was the boys' obituaries.

Tom Dorn had also died overseas—in Berzhaan.

Tory did a search on Russ Dorn. She found his contact info and was about to dial when Jay returned.

"You finished making notes for me yet?"

"Just about, Jay. I found this kid who was a child-hood friend of Garret's. I might want to do a quick interview with the father. He's a good friend of

Larry Maxwell's and they both lost their sons in the Middle East."

"We're supposed to be on a flight to D.C. in three hours."

"We can always take a later flight."

"I'm game with whatever you decide."

Tory reached for her notepad and phone but Jay's hand on her shoulder stopped her.

"What?"

"Are you okay? You look…tired."

"There's been a lot of stuff going on lately. I'm worried about Andrea."

"Something's different about you, Patton. I can't put my finger on it. But it's like you've changed."

"I have changed. I'm not the field reporter you used to know. Now I have to concentrate on anchoring a show."

"Worried about the competition?"

"I'd be a fool not to."

"Yeah, but you've always been so sure of yourself. I think this new thing with you isn't work-related."

She so didn't want to have this conversation with Jay. Not now—actually, not ever. "It's nothing. I'm just trying to get my job done and find my friend."

He gave her a searching look, but seemed to accept her words.

"I'll start editing the interview together while you make your call."

"Thanks, Jay."

"That's what they pay me for."

"No, I meant, thanks for caring."

"Can't help that."

She said nothing and just moved to the other side of the room to make her call. Tory left a message on Russ Dorn's phone. She hoped he'd call back soon, otherwise she was going to have to settle for a phone interview with him.

She heard Jay exclaim softly behind her.

"What are you doing?"

"I want to look at the hostage tape again."

"Why?"

"I'm not sure, but I think the cabin in this picture is the same one that the hostages are being held in," he said, pointing to the photo of Garret and Dorn's son that she'd paused on.

"What?"

Tory hurried across the room, her pulse pounding loudly in her ears. She waited while Jay pulled up the hostage tape and zoomed in on the window behind Cobie's head. He froze the image on the monitor and then zoomed in on the picture of the two boys. Over their shoulders was a similar window.

Tory glanced back and forth between the two

pictures one more time, seeing what Jay had spotted. There was a glass sun-catcher in the top right of the windowpane. The catcher had a Marine Corps emblem.

Not only was it in both pictures but it cast a small shadow on the floor of the tape of the hostages. A shadow that could only be seen when the tape was stopped and viewed at one frame per second.

"Hot damn. I think Mr. Maxwell didn't tell me everything."

Less than an hour later, Tory had done a deed search and come up empty. There was no hunting cabin in the Phoenix area that belonged to anyone by the name of Dorn or Maxwell.

The ringing of her cell phone interrupted her fruitless search. "Tory Patton."

"Ms. Patton, this is Russ Dorn returning your call."

His voice was low and gravelly, the kind she associated with lifelong smokers. Tory pulled her notepad closer to her. "Thanks for calling me back. I'm doing a story on Larry Maxwell and his son, Garret. I'd like to ask you a few questions about your ties to the Maxwell family."

"Why?"

She wasn't sure what she'd get from Dorn but

anything that could narrow her search would be helpful. Who was the mastermind of Freedom Now? This gravelly-voiced man, or the charming Larry Maxwell?

"My show—*A Closer Look*—focuses on stories with the human touch. I think my viewers will want to hear about the friendship your sons shared."

"I'm not sure what you want from me."

Tory had faced her share of reluctant interviewees before, and Dorn sounded as if he were going to be one of the hardest she'd ever faced.

"I'd like a chance to speak to you about your son and Garret Maxwell. They were good friends, weren't they?"

"Yes, they were. But I'm not sure how you know that. Did Larry mention me?"

Tory thought about that picture and in her mind's eye saw again that shadow on the floor of the terrorist tape. The shadow that linked both the Maxwell and Dorn families to the location where the hostages were being held. He was a link to Andrea and she wasn't going to let him go without a struggle.

She had to say the right words to make him start talking. What would they be? She wished they were face-to-face instead of on the phone, where she couldn't view his body language.

"No, sir, Mr. Maxwell didn't say anything about

you, but I noticed several pictures on the wall of Garret with your son. I also found a wonderful article on Garret and Tom and your families on the Internet."

"What pictures?" he asked.

There was something different in his voice. She paused for a second, her photographic memory easily supplying her with the details of the framed photos she'd seen. She probably shouldn't be too specific. "There were some hanging in the hallway in the Maxwell's home. One of them matched the photo used in the news article, I believe from the day the boys enlisted. Your son was excited to join the Corps, wasn't he?"

"Yes, he was. That was one of the happiest days of his life."

"You must have been proud."

"I was. I still am proud of my son. What other pictures did you notice at Larry's house?"

"Just some when the boys were younger. It made me realize that Garret and Tom knew each other for a long time."

"Larry and I go back a long ways."

"That's what I understand. I'd love to do an interview with you, Mr. Dorn. Do you have time today to speak to me?"

"I'm not sure I want to be interviewed."

"It's painless. Just me and my cameraman."

"If I do it, it'd have to be just you."

That request was one Tory had heard before. She had a small handheld camera with a tripod she could set up when she went out on her own. Considering her suspicions, they'd better meet in a public place, not Dorn's private residence. "That's fine with me. But I have to be in D.C. tomorrow for another interview. So we'd have to meet today."

"Let me think about it and call you back."

Tory knew when she was losing an interview and Mr. Dorn was slipping out of her grasp. She had no choice but to dangle the bait and see if he'd take her up on it. She and Jay could be completely off base, and the cabin would mean nothing to Dorn.

But Tory didn't believe in coincidence.

"If you won't be available, can you tell me about one of the other photos I saw at Mr. Maxwell's?"

"Which one are you curious about?" His voice sharpened.

"The picture of Garret and Tom on a hunting trip with a large buck between them."

There was a pause on the line, and she knew she was on to something. "Why that photo?"

Tory tried to think fast but she had no reason other than the fact that she suspected Andrea was in that cabin now and she wanted to know more about it. "Because you can clearly see these boys were hunters, warriors. I'd like to discuss your comment about them being too young to fight."

She heard conversation in the background, as well as some music, and wondered where Dorn was calling her from. It sounded like some roadhouse. God, she really hoped he didn't want to meet her in a bar. If he suggested a place like that, she'd have to drag Jay along.

Ben would never forgive her if she put herself in danger again. And to be honest, she wouldn't forgive herself.

"There was no call to be warriors. Larry and I hunted so the boys came with us. That's what real men do."

Tory couldn't argue with that—her father and brother hunted. "I come from a family like that."

"Do you hunt, Ms. Patton?"

"Not anymore, but growing up I did."

"Do you feel like you were called to be a warrior?" he asked, throwing her words back at her.

"No, sir. But I'm called to interview people and uncover the truth."

"You like going after the exclusive stories, don't you?"

"Yes, especially stories like this one, about people like you and Mr. Maxwell and your sons. Stories about the real American men and women who are fighting for our ideals overseas. That's why I want to talk to you. So, do you think you have the time to meet with me?"

He said nothing for a long moment and Tory held her breath waiting for his answer. This was the best lead they'd had in this story and time was running out for the hostages.

Freedom Now couldn't keep them alive forever with the government not taking action. They'd have to raise the stakes and kill someone soon to prove they were serious. And from what she'd seen of the group, they *were* serious.

"I will meet with you, Ms. Patton."

"Is there any chance you can come to the UBC affiliate station in Phoenix?" That would be entirely safe.

"I can't. But I can meet you at the Veterans of Foreign Wars Hall on the north side of Phoenix in an hour." He gave her the address.

"I'll be there."

Chapter 15

Velosi left the Watering Hole with Jones's contact and entered a big black Ford pickup truck. Ben and the rest of the LASER team lay back, waiting to see which direction they'd go. They'd left Bill Jones in the custody of the local police to be detained on suspicions of working with terrorists. Ben's CO had a lot of pull and the man wasn't afraid to use it.

Jones had been silent once they'd gotten the contact information from him. But they didn't need him to talk anymore once they knew the meeting time and place and the code. Jones had two tattoos that they'd had to recreate on Velosi. One was a black script that simply said *Jones* on his left forearm. The other was a phoenix rising from the ashes in the middle of his stomach.

Velosi was in better shape than Jones, but Ben wasn't too concerned. Velosi would just say he started working out since he'd become divorced. A piece of information they'd uncovered on William Peter Jones of Palm Springs, California.

"Salvo, did you get a photo of the contact?"

"Affirmative, boss. Running it through the computer now."

Salvo was running the picture of the man with Velosi through an international database. If their guy had a passport or priors they'd find a match.

Ben and O'Neill were in a nondescript sedan. Potchicki, Georgie and Salvo were in the Hummer.

Two vehicles would make it easier for them to trail Velosi. O'Neill had his Blackberry GPS tuned on and Ben waited for the affirmative that O'Neill had Velosi's frequency.

"Got him, sir."

"Great." The Ford truck that Velosi was in was headed northwest. Since it was summertime, the sun was a long way from setting even though it was six o'clock.

"Salvo?" Ben called the man through the wireless microphones they used.

"Go ahead."

"Are you tracking the package?" Ben asked.

"Wait a second…confirm, we have the package. Awaiting orders."

"Take the number-two position, look for stragglers as we leave. We'll switch up in a little while."

"Affirmative, sir."

Ben pulled out of the parking lot down the street and headed in the direction that O'Neill's GPS unit indicated. He was amazed sometimes at how much technology had changed his job in the last five years.

"Did you get the tag number?" Ben asked O'Neill, while they waited for a light to change.

"I'm running it now," O'Neill said.

Traffic started to move again and Ben kept the big black pickup in his sights. "The plates are registered to Tom Dorn. Give me a second and I'll—what the fuck? Dorn is dead."

"Got any more information?" Ben asked, a chill moving down his spine. This was a connection to Tory and the stories she'd been doing that he didn't want to find. He'd barely been able to make peace with the fact that she'd gone to interview the father who'd tried to kill himself.

"Georgie, you have any stragglers?"

"So far one vehicle on the street has moved. A white Bronco." He read the license plate out loud and

Ben took his eyes from the road for a minute to confirm that O'Neill had the tag number.

O'Neill nodded at him. O'Neill's computer was the latest and greatest and could run through several different databases at the same time.

"Tom Dorn died in Berzhaan about nine months ago," O'Neill said.

"Any chance his parents are part of Freedom Now?"

Ben digested that information. He'd never thought of Freedom Now being a parents' activist group. He'd considered peace protesters, or maybe some other opposition group. "Run the mother and father through your computer."

"Will do."

Ben had a chilling thought of Tory and her interview with men and women who'd lost adult children fighting against insurgents and rebels in the Middle East. If the names Petri or Maxwell came up, he was going to be seriously pissed.

She'd assured him her interviews were harmless. Did she know more than she'd told him? Or, like the LASER team, did she find out this information on the fly?

"Mother, Elizabeth 'Betty' Dorn, deceased two years ago this Christmas. She lived in nearby Palmer Junction."

"Father?" Ben asked. "Where the hell is Palmer Junction?"

"Russell Thomas Dorn, retired military. It's less than an hour outside of Phoenix. Small town, population seven hundred ninety-one."

"Is the father still alive?" Ben asked.

"Yes, sir. He lives just outside Palmer Junction. He was made mayor for a day in 2003 shortly after his wife died."

"Salvo?" Ben called for their communications guy, who was running the photo of the guy with Velosi through the computer.

"Sir?"

"Run Russell Dorn through your picture database and see if we get a match. You should be able to find a newspaper photo from 2003 in whatever the local paper in Palmer Junction, Arizona, is."

Ben followed the black pickup through traffic, careful to keep his distance. When the truck pulled off the highway and wove through a series of residential streets, Ben had to drop back and let the second team take first position.

"Target is stopping at the VFW meeting hall. The street is pretty quiet. I think you should hang back. We're going to drive by and take a position a few blocks up. We've got him in our sights," Georgie said.

"Affirmative. We're going to hang a few streets north of your position, keep me posted."

"Affirmative, sir."

He doubted that Dorn was holding the hostages in such a public place. So what the hell was he doing there? "Salvo? You got anything for me yet?"

"The target matches Dorn, sir. He's a little leaner now but it's definitely the same man."

"The second vehicle is owned by Larry Maxwell. There's a Palmer Junction address in the computer."

The man Tory was going to interview, because she thought he might be connected to Freedom Now. Damn. His first instinct was to call her and make sure she was okay, but they were in the middle of an operation and he couldn't afford any kind of distraction.

But his sexy little reporter better be safely on her way back to D.C., or else.

"What's going on, Salvo?" Ben asked.

There was total radio silence and then Salvo's voice came through. At first Ben wasn't sure he'd understood the words correctly.

"Dorn got out of the vehicle and is talking to a woman. It's Tory Patton."

Tory wasn't sure what she'd expected from Russ Dorn, but he looked different from the man she'd seen in the newspaper. His hair was shorn short in a military crew cut. His eyes were shaded with aviator-style sunglasses and he moved with the same lean and easy grace that Ben did.

She had a premonition that maybe she shouldn't have come alone. But Jay was still editing the story they'd shot earlier and Shawna had to take their scheduled flight to D.C. to get ready for tomorrow's show.

"Mr. Dorn?"

"Yes, Ms. Patton. It's a pleasure to meet you."

She shook hands with him. "I'm glad you had the time for me. Should we go inside and find a quiet table for our interview?"

"I don't have a lot of time. Let's get this over with."

That was just the kind of attitude that made for a horrible interview. "I promise this will be a painless process, Mr. Dorn."

He held the door for her as they entered. A few men were gathered at some tables in the main hall. Dorn led her to a small, quiet room in the back of the building. Unease shivered through her. But this was a better place for an interview. It would be odd to request a change.

"This is a wireless microphone." She handed it to Dorn. "Clip it to your shirt."

"What do I do with this?" he asked, indicating the black battery pack.

"You can attach it to your belt—like this," Tory said, turning around to show him. She set up the small handheld camera on the tripod and then made sure her interview section was in frame.

"If you could have a seat, Mr. Dorn."

"How's this?" he asked.

"Perfect," she said, setting the camera and taking the remote with her. It was a small wand that would allow her to start filming and also provided her with a two-inch monitor she could see to make sure both of them were in frame. On the small screen, it was impossible to tell if they were in focus or not.

"Okay, we're ready to start. Do you need a glass of water?"

He shook his head. Tory took a bottle of water from her own bag and took a few swallows before turning back to Dorn.

"I'm going to start with a few questions about Larry and Garret Maxwell and then ask you to tell me about your son, Tom."

He nodded, a brisk military shake, and Tory tried to think of something she could do to relax this man. She hit the record button, turned to face the camera fully and smiled.

"I'm here at the VFW Hall in Phoenix, Arizona

with Mr. Russ Dorn, retired Marine Corps Lance Corporal. He shares a friendship with Larry Maxwell that stretches back more than twenty years. But that's not all these two men share—they also share the loss of their sons during military service in the Middle East."

Tory turned to Mr. Dorn. "Tell me a little about your family and the Maxwells."

He cleared his throat. "I met Larry in 'Nam. We were from the same area of the country, and when we got out we both moved to Palmer Junction to settle down."

"That's where you raised your sons."

"Yes, ma'am. We took vacations together."

"Hunting trips?"

"Yes, and camping, and white-water rafting trips, stuff like that," he said.

Tory wanted to get back to the hunting cabin, but Dorn had moved on so she couldn't probe for a location like she wanted to.

Thinking of the pictures they had from Maxwell's house that they could use on the screen during the interview, Tory decided to ask about Tom Dorn's military career. "They also went together to a recruiting office here in Phoenix to join the Marines."

"Yes, they did. I raised my son as a proud

American and he couldn't stay at home when he could serve his country."

Tory tipped her head to the side. This was a different attitude than Larry Maxwell had. "You supported his desire to go overseas and fight for his country."

"Damn straight I did."

"When you learned of you son's death, did that change your attitude?"

Dorn got quiet and still, looking away from her and the camera for a long moment. "I was still proud of my boy. That will never change. But I did have questions about the meaning of his death. What had changed by his giving his life?"

"Who did you seek answers from?" she asked.

"The government and former President Whitlow. More recently from President Monihan."

"What did he say?"

"Nothing but a load of BS. I got a letter honoring Tommy, but I still didn't see where his dying had made life better for anyone."

The interview was turning a little hostile, and though that made good television—viewers loved to see strong emotion—she didn't want to end the interview until she could get a little more information from him.

"Where was Tom serving?"

"In Berzhaan."

"How did he die?"

"A skirmish with Kemeni forces, outside Suwan. He shouldn't even have been there. He was assigned a post at the U.S. embassy. But several soldiers on recon got sick, and Tom volunteered to fill in."

"I was recently in Suwan. It seems that the breakdown of the Kemeni rebels' power in that country has left it a safer place."

"Not too safe. that's where the American hostages were taken. And suicide bombers are still blowing things up."

"True. But your son helped make life safer for families, for mothers and children in that country, in a way it wasn't before."

"You might have a point."

She wasn't going to get a good sound bite from Dorn because he wasn't the kind of man to speak in fifteen-second chunks. "Are you familiar with Military Parents in Support of Withdrawal Now?"

"Yes. I participated in a protest walk with the group on Memorial Day."

"Are you still a member of the group?"

"Yes."

"Have you heard of Freedom Now?"

"Yes, ma'am."

"Are you a member of that group?" Tory asked.

Russ watched her for a minute and Tory felt fear close her throat. What the hell had she been thinking to ask that? She knew better than to throw something like that out there.

"Aren't they the group that took the hostages?"

"Yes," Tory said.

"No, I'm not a part of that group."

There was a ring of conviction in his voice and in his eyes, but Tory couldn't shake the feeling, as she put away the microphones and the camera, that she'd put herself in danger with those questions.

Dorn left before she did, and Tory breathed a sigh of relief. She'd have to call their research department for a wild card search on Dorn and Freedom Now, but she was only working on this story on a limited basis. Ben's team was checking out Larry Maxwell. Maybe they would be able to get some answers on Dorn. Because there was something going on with that man.

When she called Ben, his phone went straight to voice mail.

"Hey, it's me. I've got a new name for you to look into. Russ Dorn. He served with Larry Maxwell, and his son died in Berzhaan."

She disconnected the call and put her cell phone away. Maybe she should try to tail Dorn and see where he went. Keep her distance but follow him. She sent a quick text message to Shawna, telling her she was going to take the last flight out and that she was investigating a lead on Andrea and the other hostages.

Russ lurked outside the door, listening. Tory Patton and her damned nosy questions really pissed him off. There was no way that he could let her go back and air that story asking him if he was part of Freedom Now. Too many people would start looking at him and Larry and their connection.

A fourth hostage was the last thing he wanted. But he couldn't let Patton leave. He had a contingency plan for just this scenario.

The hunting cabin had been Betty's, and was in his wife's maiden name, but a nosy broad like Patton wouldn't let that stop her from finding it. And he wasn't leaving any loose ends.

Quietly he called Larry on his cell and told him to put the plan in motion. Larry would distract the vets with a flag-lowering ceremony for his son while Russ subdued Patton. She was a petite woman— should be no trouble.

A mission only worked when the man in charge controlled all avenues. Even those that spelled failure. He tensed as Patton packed her gear and stood. He'd left the door open and could hear the click of her shoes as she approached.

As soon as she stepped through the doorway, he grabbed the back of her blouse at the base of her neck with his left hand. She shrugged in his grip, lashing backward with a strong kick that connected with his thigh.

"Let me go!"

"I don't think so."

She shrieked and he brought his right hand across her throat, trying to shut her up. She twisted in his grip, bringing her heel down on his instep.

"Help!" she screamed.

He tightened his grip on her throat, closing off her airway. Eventually she went limp, her slight body slumping in his arms. He started to loosen his grip and she twisted again. He put his left hand on her forehead, securing her in a headlock and pulling her backward to force her off balance.

She screamed again and he put his palm over her mouth and nose. "If you don't want to die, shut up." He prayed Larry had succeeded in luring everyone from the main hall. So far no one had run to the rescue, a good sign.

Her eyes widened. He stepped back and went down on his left knee, keeping the headlock secure. She reached up, gouging her nails across his face. He brought his right leg over her left arm and pulled it back to restrain her.

She dug her nails into his lower calf. Her fingers scored the skin through the fabric of his pants. She flailed in his arms until he leaned forward, using his body weight to bring her under control. He rolled her onto her stomach, keeping the headlock secure. He let go of her forehead and pulled her hands behind her back.

He used his belt to bind her hands. Then he took his handkerchief from his pocket and stuffed it in her mouth.

He pulled her to her feet, gathered up her bag and dragged her down the hallway toward the back door just as he heard the front door of the VFW Hall open and footsteps tromp back inside.

Larry was waiting for him. "Take her."

Larry tossed Tory over his shoulder and Russ double-checked to make sure nothing was left.

Russ didn't think of anything except getting back to the cabin where there would be nothing unforeseen. He climbed into his own pickup truck and slowly drove out of the parking lot.

He glanced in the backseat of his extended cab where Bill Jones was trussed up and met the man's eyes. "Sorry about the restraints. Until we get to where we're going, it's better if you lay low."

The man grunted something but Russ didn't pay any attention. He turned on the radio, flipping to the all-news channel that he kept programmed on number three.

There was nothing new in relation to the government and the action they were taking to get back the hostages. What would it take for this government to act? Would the two new missing people, Bill Jones and the reporter Tory Patton, be enough to force some kind of action? Freedom Now would have to send a new video with the original hostages bodies.

When he'd first come up with this plan, the idea had seemed so totally infallible. Now, he became more and more convinced that nothing would get through the barrier the president had erected around himself and his position on the military need for American troops in the Middle East. But he wouldn't give up.

He breathed deeply, tapping into the part of his soul that had been at war. The part of his soul that knew what it was like to take a life. The part that would have to take over once again.

Because a grieving father couldn't inflict that kind of pain on another parent. A grieving father couldn't clear his head of the children who'd once played with his own deceased son. A grieving father was a liability in a battle where only the strong could survive.

The sun sank slowly below the horizon and Russ

flipped on his lights, tossing his sunglasses on the dashboard. Something changed inside him. A settling of what was past and present, coming together to form some kind of person capable of claiming the future he wanted. The future he needed. The future as he would make it.

He braked to a stop and reached back to untie Bill Jones's hands and remove the gag. "Climb up front if you want. We're almost there."

"What the *hell* was that about?" Jones asked.

"I thought I made it clear in the bar. This is a job where you are required to take orders and follow them. You said you understood."

"I do understand. I'm good at taking orders, but being bound in the back of a truck for almost three hours...that I didn't sign up for."

"It was either keep you in the dark as to where we're located or kill you after you see to our patients."

Jones didn't flinch or pale, he simply sat a little straighter in his seat. "Then I guess a word of thanks is in order."

Russ said nothing else. He didn't give a damn what the man thought of him. If Jones proved himself in the cabin then the man would live and leave in the morning. If he didn't, then so be it. Russ knew better than to force his will on someone else.

Every man had to live with his decisions and the consequences of those decisions. He was sure Bill Jones would make the choice that was right for him. Rodney and Jake should be back from D.C. now—he could have them deal with Jones.

"What am I going to be treating?"

"Like I said in the e-mail, gangrene and some dehydration. Your patients have been drugged for almost ten days now and we're not sure of the long-term effects."

"What drug?"

"Valium."

"Valium?"

"Yes. It keeps them groggy and out of it."

"There's just the three, right?"

"Actually, we have four now, but one of them is new and I'm not sure how we'll deal with her."

Russ parked behind the cabin and led Bill Jones inside. The other man paused in the doorway, surveying the small room and assessing the occupants with his pale eyes.

Was it Russ's imagination, or did Jones jump slightly when Tory Patton was brought in and dumped on the floor?

Chapter 16

Tory woke with a start. Dull pain throbbed at the base of her neck and her stomach felt like one big bruise. She panicked for a second, worry about her unborn child swamping her. Then her Athena Academy training kicked in and she pushed aside her worry.

Any child of hers and Ben's would have a strong will to survive. But she needed to get to a doctor as quickly as possible. She kept her eyes closed and listened for voices. She heard nothing but the loud sound of a ticking clock and the shuffle of footsteps over a hardwood floor.

She opened her eyes as little as possible, trying

to figure out the best way to take control of her current situation. Her hands were bound behind her back and she flexed her fingers around the thick, stiff binding. It felt smooth on one side, rough on the other. Maybe a leather belt?

Her feet were bound and a handkerchief was stuffed in her mouth. She worked her jaw carefully, using her tongue to push the cloth out of her mouth. Her head ached badly enough that she could hear her own racing heartbeat echoing through it.

The room she was in was lit with an overhead lamp. She turned her head to the left and saw Andrea and Cobie and the third man…Paul Manning. She'd found her friend but she wasn't sure what good she was going to do her. She took heart in the fact that she'd left a voice mail for Ben, giving him Russ's name, but she had no idea if he'd be able to find this remote location.

She'd searched the deed records and spent the little time she could trying to figure out who owned the cabin, to no avail. But maybe with his endless database resources, he'd find something she hadn't.

Still, she couldn't wait to be rescued. Especially since she knew time was running out. She'd figure this out. If Andrea were conscious, her friend would be a good partner in getting them all out of here.

She glanced at the three hostages. Their clothes were dirty and ripped, their faces pale and their lips white and cracked. Tory wasn't too sure they'd be able to walk out of this cabin on their own. She skimmed the room with her gaze, looking for something she could use. Of course, maybe she should get herself free first.

She steadily worked her hands against the bonds, knowing that nothing other than slow and steady movements would work to free her.

She pushed herself into a sitting position. And felt her stomach rebel.

"Good. You're awake."

Startled, she turned to the left and for the first time noticed the man sitting there. He looked familiar somehow. He wore his dark brown hair longish, brushing his collar. He had on chinos and a Santa Cruz Surf competition shirt. His forearm had a tattoo that said Jones. Hmm. That didn't ring a bell.

She tried to speak but felt bile well up in her throat and she turned away, throwing up. She shook and felt moisture on her face. The man didn't move, just sat on his haunches staring at her. She wiped her face on her shoulders.

"I don't know if there's anything good about it," Tory croaked. "Should I ask who you are?"

"Bill Jones, EMT."

"Can I have a sip of water to rinse my mouth?" she asked.

He walked across the room, filled a tin cup with water and brought it back to her. He held the cup to her mouth. She swished it and looked around for a place to spit, finally just spitting back into the tin cup.

"Thank you."

He didn't respond, just went back across the room and emptied the cup into the sink. He returned to her side, placing two fingers against her wrist, no doubt taking her pulse.

"My heart rate is going to be accelerated." She knew it. She hoped she wasn't in shock. That would seriously slow down any escape/rescue attempt. But if she knew her physical limitations she could factor them into her planning.

"I think that's an understatement," he said. He dug around in his medical bag and removed a small bottle of liquid medicine and a syringe.

"I'm pregnant."

His hand jerked from where he'd been about to draw the medicine into the syringe. "Why are you telling me this?"

"I don't know the effects of whatever that drug is on my baby."

He studied the label for a quick minute and then turned back to her. "I have no idea, either."

"Could you not inject me until you find out?" she

asked him. She realized that her pregnancy might aid her in gaining the sympathy of this man, who was part of an organization dedicated to saving adult children.

"Please. I was in an…altercation earlier."

"What kind of altercation?" he asked.

He had kind, worried eyes for a bad guy, she thought. But then he probably didn't think of himself as a villain. He believed in his cause and in doing whatever needed to be done. The ends justifying the means.

"A fight with a man. My stomach is really sore. Do you think my baby is okay?" she asked.

He put his hand on her shoulder. "Are you bleeding or spotting?"

"I kind of just woke up. Maybe you could untie my hands and I could go check."

He gave her a wry smile, arching one eyebrow at her. "I'm not that gullible."

Something about his voice teased her memory. She just couldn't place it. Well, she needed an ally in the cabin and right now Bill was her only shot. "I didn't think you were. Someone could guard me."

"Let me check with Dorn and I'll let you know."

"How are the others?" she asked. "They don't look very good."

"They're all a little dehydrated. There are

numerous signs of exhaustion, but no broken bones or internal injuries. The guy without the fingertip has an infection, but I've given him an antibiotic that should fix that. I've also given everyone a tetanus shot."

She shifted around. "Is the cavalry here?"

"Not yet," he said, under his breath, and her heart leapt.

The front door opened and Russ Dorn walked in, followed by Larry and two other men that Tory had never spoken to before. The blond man looked even more familiar to her then Jones did. Where did she know these men from?

Tory leaned back against the wall, staying as still and quiet as possible while running the blond man's face through her mind and trying to place him. She knew him from a recent interview she'd done. Not with him, but they'd used his picture...*Rodney Petri.* Janice's ex-husband.

Ben and his men waited less than a mile from Velosi, dressed in desert camouflage. His GPS beacon had stopped moving over two hours ago and it was completely dark in the desert.

Tension strung Ben's shoulders tight. They'd had no choice but to follow Dorn and Maxwell when they'd seen their vehicles leave the VFW, but Ben hadn't seen Tory get into her car. Although Dorn had come out of the front of the VFW, likely while Tory was still packing up, Ben would feel better if he'd actually seen her get into her car and drive away. She'd left him the message to check out Dorn after finishing the interview, so Dorn must have already been gone. Still…he worried.

The LASER team had used satellite thermal heat images to determine that there were seven bodies in the cabin below them. Four of the bodies weren't moving and were clumped together by the north-facing wall. There were two other bodies in a separate area, which Ben and O'Neill had determined was a second room.

Ben hoped that Velosi wasn't incapacitated. But they had a contingency plan for rescuing Velosi as well.

They'd used the information Tory provided over voice mail to confirm that Russ Dorn was indeed the owner of the cabin below.

It was time for their in-briefing. He also had to make sure the team understood the rules of engagement. Ben's CO had been emphatic that he didn't want a Rambo-style bloodbath after the hostages were rescued, and Ben agreed.

"We'll go in quiet and quick. There are four targets," Ben said, restating the mission objective for the men. Salvo dispensed wireless radio earpieces to each of them. "Georgie and Potchicki you will provide cover from there." He indicated a small ridge less than fifty feet from the cabin.

"Salvo, how many sentries did you observe?" Ben asked. He'd had Salvo keep watch while the snipers had been scouting for a good location to set up.

"A two-man unit, sir. They make rounds every forty minutes. We should be able to slip by them without notice."

"I think we should take them out. So we don't have to worry about them," O'Neill said.

Ben felt the tension in this group. They wanted their two team members back and he knew they were ready for blood. They'd been waiting all day for action and now they were ready to move. He was, too. He wanted Manning and Velosi safe, and Andrea and Cobie back in Manhattan where they belonged. And then he wanted to take his leave so he could convince Tory to marry him.

"Agreed. We'll take them on the way in." The smoother and quicker they could get this done, the better for all involved.

"We're going in soft," Ben said to his men. "You need a confirmation before you make a kill. Is that understood?"

"Yes, sir."

"Let's check our radios and then we'll move out."
Ben waited until he was sure each man had placed
the earbud in his ear.

"This is one," Ben said.

"Two," O'Neill said.

"Three," Salvo said.

"Four," Potchicki said.

"Five," Georgie said.

"We'll be on silent until we subdue the targets.
O'Neill, I want you to come in from the north and
take care of the sentry patrolling that side.

"Salvo, you cover us from the west. Georgie and
Potchicki, you'll cover the road leading into the
cabin from the ridge."

"I'll take out the guard on the south side. Let's
move out."

The men fanned out in the area surrounding the
small hunting cabin. The moon had risen and was
full giving them too much exposure to just maneuver
closer to the building. They were all on their bellies,
inching their way closer to the cabin.

A small chirping sounded in Ben's ear and he ac-
knowledged the signal from the sniper team that
they were in position.

Ben shifted to his knees as one of the sentries
neared his position. He used the saguaro cactus and

desert brush for cover. He saw Salvo out of the corner of his eye, but Ben signaled that he could handle the guard on his own.

Ben came up from his knees and wrapping one arm around the guard's throat, closing off his carotid arteries. The guard wrapped his hands around Ben's wrists and flailed, but soon passed out. Ben secured him with wrist and ankle cuffs.

Then he dragged the man deeper into the brush and continued moving forward to the cabin. Each man chirped softly when they were in position. Ben sat quietly under the window, listening to the voices. He identified Velosi's voice first and was glad that their man wasn't out of commission.

A soft breeze blew through the night and Ben used the sound for cover as he shifted his weight and stood in the darkness to the left of the window. He saw the shadows of four men moving in the cabin, then scanned the interior, finding Velosi on his knees, tending to a patient.

Not one of the three hostages though. Manning and the two UBC news people lay against the wall, bound, a few feet from the medic. Ben glanced back at Velosi but couldn't see around the man to identify the fourth person.

He recognized Larry Maxwell and Russ Dorn. The other two men in the room weren't familiar to him.

"You about done, Jones?" Dorn asked.

"Yes, sir. I'm checking the last one now."

"How are they? Does that boy have gangrene?"

"No, at least I don't think so. The rest of them aren't in the best shape they've ever been in, but I think they'll live," Velosi said. "This one is pregnant and has asked to use the bathroom to make sure there wasn't any damage done to the fetus during her fight with you."

Ben's blood chilled as he heard those words. He knew it was Tory even before Velosi stood, revealing her.

"Pregnant?" Dorn glared down at the person sitting next to Velosi.

"Yes, Mr. Dorn."

The sound of her feminine voice, soft and smooth, rushed through his mind. A hint of the South warmed that standard newscaster's drawl. *Dammit.*

Tory stopped trying to free her hands and waited to see if Dorn was going to let her use the restroom. She figured that could give her some sort of advantage.

"Where did she come from?" Rodney Petri asked.

"She was asking nosy questions. We couldn't afford to leave her in Phoenix."

"I don't like this."

"I don't care."

Rodney backed away from Russ, putting his hands up. "Whatever. What are we going to do with her?"

"Keep her sedated like the rest of them."

Jones came back to her side, the syringe in his hand.

"Wait!" Tory cried. "Drugs can be very harmful to babies at this early stage."

Jones hesitated, clearly waiting to see if she'd sway Dorn into not drugging her. She kept working on her hands behind her back. If she had her hands free, she'd at least have a fighting chance.

"Rodney and Jake, go outside and get the boxes ready," Russ ordered.

Tory watched the two men leave, still working to free her hands. Her wrists felt raw and they burned each time she slid them against the leather, but she didn't stop working.

Thinking about what she knew of both of Dorn and Maxwell, she tried to come up with something she could say to sway them. To make them release the hostages. She had taken an online class in hostage negotiation a long time ago.

She tried to place herself in both men's shoes. How would she feel if her child were killed fighting for a cause she didn't believe in? It was hard to imagine what her baby would look like, much less think of her child dying. Ben's face floated through her mind. It was easy to conceive that he might be killed someday.

"Tell me what you hope to accomplish by doing this," Tory said. "The government hasn't responded to your demands and everyone I talked to in the Pentagon didn't think that time would convince our government to act. Maybe there's something I can do using my media connections."

"The media attention doesn't help, Ms. Patton. Janice has been on every show that would have her for more than six months, and nothing is happening. We've lobbied the House and the Senate and our troops are still dying in the Middle East."

"You just need to get public sentiment on your side," Tory said, realizing she understood these men. If the world were a peaceful place then Ben would never have to go out on an assignment again. But she also knew that in reality, there would always be some war to fight.

"I think we both know it's too late for that. We went into this with our eyes open."

Tory didn't think that statement was true but she wasn't going to argue with the man holding her captive. She wanted him to relax. To think of her as the face that many Americans knew from her years as a reporter.

"Hurting me and my baby isn't going to help your cause at all. Violence is never a solution, you must know that. Your son's death is what triggered these actions."

"Violence is the only thing that some men understand, Ms. Patton. Men like President Monihan. Letter-writing campaigns don't work. Threats don't work. Violence is the only thing we have left."

She noticed the weapons held loosely in Russ's and Larry's hands for the first time. She had been so focused on getting free she hadn't realized she was talking to men who had already decided on a course of action.

She took a deep breath, keeping herself calm. "I think you're selling yourself short—both of you. The men I interviewed aren't cold-blooded killers," Tory said, including Larry in her stare, hoping that one of the men could be swayed to letting her and the hostages go.

Bill stayed quietly in the background, probably afraid that if he said something that either man didn't like he'd end up dead like the hostages. Like herself. Tory had always been a good conversationalist, able to keep any conversation going. Always been a top-notch reporter, able to coax the most reticent person into sharing their innermost feelings. Always been a talker, and now she was talking to save her life.

"We are killers. We fought in Vietnam and killed for our country. We killed to keep our families safe and that didn't do any of our sons much good, did it?"

"Those boys were fighting for the same things you fought for. Don't make less of their sacrifice," Tory said. "Remember that picture on Larry's wall of Garret and Tom on the day they joined the Corps? Those were men who were excited to be part of something. Excited to fight for their country."

Russ rubbed the back of his neck. "I'm not sure what your point is. We've already decided what we're going to do, Ms. Patton, and nothing you say is going to change our minds."

"I understand that. Have you thought about calling the government to talk instead of sending another fingertip?"

"We're not sending another fingertip—we're sending a body. Then we'll call to make sure they received it."

Tory's blood chilled at the way that Russ made that last statement. She realized at once that this wasn't the grieving father she'd interviewed earlier. This was a man much like Ben was whenever she encountered him undercover. A man on a mission who was sure of his objectives and planned to stay the course.

"Please, Russ. Those hostages are people's sons and daughters."

Tory tried to recall everything she knew about the three people. Andrea and Cobie she knew and had worked with, but Paul she had never met. And the details she'd uncovered about him had been scant.

"Andrea's father died two years ago, and she's helping to support her mother and younger sister. Cobie's family has already had a lot of stress from the finger you sent. Paul is a good guy who spends his time volunteering in children's shelters," Tory said, making up the last bit and promising God that if He got them out of this, she'd make sure that Paul did some volunteering.

"You just named people I don't know. I look at these three and I see woman hostage and male hostage one, male hostage two. These aren't people anymore, not to me. To me, they're the leverage I need to get what I want."

She wanted to scream that he was being selfish. But she didn't. "How do you think these parents are going to feel when they have to visit their children at the cemetery? How do you feel when you visit your son's grave?"

Russ said nothing, just glared at her. "Jones?"

"Yes?"

"Take her to the bathroom and then sedate her."

Tory knew she'd pushed too hard. But didn't regret it. Russ was determined to take someone's life tonight and she was just as determined that he wouldn't.

Bill bent and untied her feet and then helped her to stand before leading her to a small bathroom. "Make it quick."

"Will you untie my hands?" Tory asked. He put a hand on her shoulder and spun her around. She felt the bindings on her wrists loosen and then slide away.

Tory stepped into the bathroom, closing the door before he got any ideas about making her keep it open. She closed her eyes and tried to think of what she was going to do next. When she opened them, Ben was standing directly in front of her.

Chapter 17

Tory wrapped her arms around Ben, hugging him to her for just a quick minute. She almost lost her composure seeing him here when the odds were so stacked against her and her friends.

He wore desert camouflage and some paint on his face and looked like a heroic warrior. She knew this was just another glimpse of the man she loved.

But then she pushed away from him to stare up into his eyes. She needed to pass as much information to him as she could before Bill came back and told her that her time was up in the bathroom.

"The hostages can't make it out on their own,

they're drugged and weak. Two men are outside in the yard. Did you get them?"

Ben rubbed his finger down the side of her face. She flinched as he encountered a bruise she hadn't realized she had.

"Yes, we got them," he said in the soundless way he had of talking when he was undercover. He pulled her to him and gently kissed the bruised area of her face. She felt so cherished and safe with him here, like she now had a second wind. With Ben by her side she knew they would free the hostages and get the bad guys.

"Good. Larry and Russ are in this main room with an EMT guy. How many men do you have with you?" she asked. She liked to know the odds. She was sure that Ben had a plan to rescue the hostages and she didn't want to get in his way.

"That EMT guy is on my team. You might have glimpsed him the night we were attacked in Berzhaan," Ben said. "You have more bumps and bruises than I like to see on you."

"That's fine, because I'm one big ache." She swallowed hard. She still wasn't sure that the baby was okay. "I don't know if anything happened to the baby when Russ abducted me."

Ben pulled her back into his arms. "That book

I've been reading says that babies are pretty well-insulated in the womb."

She wasn't sure if he was telling the truth or just lying to make her feel better. Then she glanced into his eyes and saw the truth there. They were partners in this, and he wasn't going to lie even to make her feel better.

"What are you doing here?" he whispered, against her temple.

"I asked to use the bathroom to get my hands free," she said. "In fact, I really do have to go. Turn around."

He turned away from her and she used the toilet, noting that there was no blood in her urine. What Ben had read about babies must be true. She washed her hands and he turned back to face her.

"I meant, what are you doing in this cabin? I thought you were interviewing Maxwell outside of Phoenix."

"I was." She explained making the connection between Maxwell and Dorn through their sons.

"You're too smart for your own good," he said, gruffly. "Do you have your hunting knife?"

"No. I was on an interview, remember?" She felt so silly that she hadn't been prepared. Ben removed his knife sheath and handed the weapon to Tory. She tucked it into the back of her pants.

"Do you want a handgun?" he asked, holding out a small semiautomatic.

She shook her head. "My arm is still sore from

where Russ used it to overpower me earlier. I'm better with the knife."

Ben rubbed her arm, a strong massaging motion that hurt at first but then lessened the pain in her arm. "When we get out of here, I'll take all your pain away."

"Hurry it up in there," Bill called through the door, pounding on it for emphasis.

Tory jumped, then remembered "Bill" was on their side.

"How did you get a man in here?" she whispered, amazed at how good Ben was at his job. She'd always had that knowledge but seeing him in action brought everything home. She couldn't ask him to stop doing what he did, because he was very good at it and what he did meant something. Not just because this time he was rescuing her friend, but because he really did save lives and save families.

"I'll tell you everything later. For now, go back out there and stay out of the way."

"I'm sorry, but are you telling me to wait for you to rescue me?"

"No, definitely not. Just don't give us away until we're ready."

"When you make your move I'll free the hostages and get them out. Did your EMT guy bring a drug that will wake them up?"

"Yes."

Tory opened the door and Bill stood there, blocking the view of the room. "Took you long enough."

"Sorry about that," she said. "I figured this was going to be my only chance to use the facilities."

Ben communicated with Bill over her shoulder, giving the man some sort of hand signal. "Turn around so I can tie your hands again."

He leaned close as he bound her hands, this time with some cord instead of the belt.

Larry Maxwell stood near the back doorway, a pine casket and body bag on the floor next to him. A chill spread through Tory's body as she noticed those items. All of her talk hadn't meant a thing to Dorn. He wasn't going to be swayed.

"It's a nice and easy bow. Just pull the string," Bill whispered in her ear.

"Come on, Rodney, what the hell is taking you so long?" Larry asked.

Tory was glad the hostages were unconscious. Somehow she didn't think it would do them any good to have to speculate which one of them would be going to D.C. to force the government to act.

Hauling her by the arm, "Bill" dragged her back across the room and pushed her to the floor, closer to the hostages this time.

Russ came out of the office, his Russian handgun held loosely in his right hand. "What's going on?"

Larry gestured toward the open doorway. "Rodney and Jake haven't come back."

"Go look for them. Bill and I will keep an eye on the hostages."

Bill knelt in front of her to tie her feet together. "Stay low. Everything's going to happen quickly."

Ben drew his Sig-Sauer and eased the bathroom door partially open. Velosi hadn't closed the door all the way. Ben moved into position, waiting. This was the hardest part. He heard the whoosh and swish of a bullet being fired from a silencer and then the thump of a body.

Ben waited for the chirping signal of his men. As soon as he heard it he opened the door and stepped into the room with his weapon drawn.

Russ glanced at Ben in full desert camouflage and face paint. In seeming slow motion he checked his hostages and then looked over at Tory, obviously coming to the conclusion that she was the one responsible for this.

"If he shoots me, kill the reporter, Jones," Russ ordered.

Ben fired at Dorn's gun arm, causing him to drop his weapon.

Dorn yelled and grabbed another weapon from his boot, shooting Velosi before Ben could stop it.

"Oh, God, you killed him," Tory screamed.

Dorn was distracted by Tory's scream. Ben moved quickly to Dorn's right side and turned sideways. Leading with his left foot, he stepped diagonally toward Dorn, keeping his shooting arm directly in front of him. He grabbed Dorn's wrist with his left hand, bringing his weapon up toward Dorn's face.

Dorn brought his left hand up in a cross-cut punch that knocked Ben's head back. Ben held tight to Dorn's wrist. The other man hit him again, pivoting on his left foot and breaking Ben's grip on his arm.

Ben went in low, kicking the weapon out of Dorn's reach. Dorn scrambled for his weapon. He palmed his gun and rolled to his feet, bringing his weapon up.

Ben fired, aiming again for Dorn's gun hand. Dorn fired at the same instant; Ben turned sideways to present as small a target as possible and felt the bullet enter the fleshy part of his upper arm.

Ben approached from Dorn's left side, striking his right arm and bringing his body around with a circular motion. He took Dorn's elbow with his left hand, using it to force Dorn's hand toward the ground, and not stopping the motion until Dorn lay on the floor at his feet.

Ben forced Dorn over onto his stomach and brought both of Dorn's hands together behind his back, binding them with a zip cord from his pocket. His entire body ached from head to toe, but when Tory sank down next to him, her small arms wrapping around his waist, he felt a wave of peace wash over him.

"Game's over, Dorn."

Tory Patton was having a great day. She sank deeper into the hot tub that was filled with bubbles. She'd gotten praise from her boss at UBC for the story she'd filed tonight on Freedom Now.

Using the interviews she'd done with Larry Maxwell and Russ Dorn, she'd edited the story together with some footage she'd shot herself of the two men being brought into custody along with Rodney Petri and Jake Brittan.

She knew her story had a sympathetic feel toward Dorn and Maxwell, but Tory had understood the men and what they'd hoped to accomplish. That didn't mean she agreed with anything they'd done to achieve their objectives.

Ben had gone to D.C. to tie up loose ends on this latest mission and for a debriefing, but he was coming to Manhattan tonight. Tory had arranged to have the next three days off. Tyson said she deserved it after going above and beyond for her exclusive interview.

She leaned her head back against the padded terry-cloth pillow and let the warm water sooth her aching body. Her doctor had given her a clean bill of health. Both she and the baby were fine. Tory put her hands on her stomach, wishing she could touch her child.

"Is this a private party?" Ben asked from the doorway. She smiled and looked up. It felt like eons since they'd left each other in Arizona.

"No, but it is by invitation only."

"Am I invited?" Ben asked.

"I don't know. Are you going to give me another lecture about staying out of trouble?"

"Yes. But not while you're lying naked in the tub."

"Hmm…so the way around lectures is simply to stay naked."

Ben grinned at her as he unbuttoned his shirt and tossed it aside. She caught her breath at the sight of his chest. He was so toned and muscular. A perfect male specimen. And he was hers. She knew that now. Tonight she planned to accept his marriage proposal.

"I'm a jealous man, babe. So if you're going to be naked, you'll have to stay at home all the time." He toed off his shoes and socks.

"Keep calling me *babe* and you're invitation to this private party is going to be revoked."

"Think you can kick me out?"

"Hopefully it won't come to that. You're a smart man. I trust you to start showing me some respect."

"Sweetheart, you know I have nothing but respect for you."

He unfastened his pants and pushed them down his legs, then stood totally naked in front of her. His erection stuck straight out from his body.

"I'm not sure that's respect," she said, eyeing his arousal. Her body got shivery just from this visual evidence of how much he wanted her.

"It's more than respect," he said, stepping into the tub. The hair on his legs brushed against her shoulder. She kissed his thigh and his hands came down, tangling in her hair. "Scoot forward so I can sit behind you."

She slid up and Ben settled in behind her. Waves rippled from the movement, splashing over the side of the tub.

He pulled her back against his chest and wrapped his arms around her waist, and she tipped her head back to look up at him.

He leaned down, rubbing his lips over hers, slowly seducing her mouth, tracing the seam between them with his tongue and then slipping it inside.

"Damn, I missed you."

"Me, too. How's Velosi?"

"Good. He's expected to make a full recovery. He said to thank you for your first-aid. The doctor said that you saved his life."

"You were the one who knew what to do. How did you get him in there anyway?"

"I don't want to talk about work tonight."

"You don't? What do you want to talk about, Ben?"

"You and me," he said, his hands sliding down her body and settling on her stomach. "Our child."

"Did you get my voice mail? My doctor said the baby is totally fine. No side effects from the fight with Dorn."

"Yes, I did. I think *I'm* still having some side effects from that."

"You promised if I was naked there wouldn't be another lecture."

"That's right, I did. But I can't really see much of your naked body."

Tory shifted around so she was facing him, rising up to her knees. She felt the water and soap suds sliding down her body, baring her breasts to his gaze. Her nipples hardened as the cooler air brushed over her skin.

"Is this better?"

"Hell, yeah. Come here woman," he said, taking her by the waist and lifting her onto his lap. His teeth scraped against her breast before he found her nipple and suckled her.

She arched her back, her hands tunneling through his hair, holding him to her. She felt a liquid response to his caresses deep inside her body.

His hands slid up and down her back and his erection nudging at her center. She reached between their bodies and positioned the tip of his cock at her entrance.

"Not yet, Tory," he said, lifting her off his body and standing with her in his arms.

Ben carried her back to their bed and made love to her. He hesitated as he was about to enter her body. "I want us to be a real family."

With his naked erection at the portal of her body, it took a second for her to understand what she was asking. "Are you waiting for me to say I'll marry you?"

He leaned down and kissed her tenderly. He lay down on top of her and she put her hands on his chest, holding him back from entering her body.

"Yes," he said, bending down to capture the tip of her breast in his mouth. He sucked her deep in his mouth, his teeth lightly scraping against her sensitive flesh. His other hand played at her other breast, arousing her, making her arch against him in need.

"Now, Ben. I can't wait."

"I haven't heard the answer I'm waiting for."

She reached between them and took his erection in her hand, bringing him closer to her. Spreading her legs wider so that she was totally open to him. "I need you, now and forever."

He lifted his head. The tips of her breasts were damp from his mouth and felt very tight. He rubbed his chest over them before sliding deep into her body.

She wanted to close her eyes as he made love to her. To somehow keep him from seeing how susceptible she was to him, but then she saw the way he watched her, knew that he felt the same way she did. That together they were each other's strength and weakness.

She slid her hands down his back, cupping his butt as he thrust deeper into her. Their eyes met, making her feel as if their souls were meeting. She felt her body start to tighten around him, catching her by surprise. She climaxed before him. He gripped her hips, holding her down and thrusting into her two more times before he came with a loud groan of her name.

He held her afterward, pulling her into his arms and tucking her up against his side.

She wrapped her arm around him and listened to the solid beating of his heart.

"I hope that was a yes."

"Of course it was a yes. I was afraid of depending on you too much, Ben. Afraid that somehow you would change me somehow."

"I never want to change you."

"But you already have…you make me a stronger person. You've forced me out of my world where I'm in total control and made me realize how much fuller my life is now."

"I love you, babe."

"I love you, too."

* * * * *

Don't miss the **ATHENA FORCE** *adventure*
Pawn
by Carla Cassidy.
Available in January 2007
wherever Silhouette Books are sold.

1206/18a

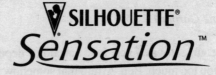

THE HEART OF A RULER by Marie Ferrarella

Capturing the Crown

Princess Amelia's arranged marriage is called off when her royal fiancé is found murdered…and the only suspect is the man she spent a wild night of passion with, After the King announces Lord Russell as the next in line to the throne, Amelia is torn between her duty and loving a suspected killer.

HARD CASE COWBOY by Nina Bruhns

No one ran faster from love than ranch foreman Redhawk Jackson, until Rhiannon O'Bronach arrived and made working together a necessity—and a sweet torture. As they ran the ranch and dealt with its hardship, Redhawk began to wonder if this tough-as-nails woman was a threat to his future…or the key to his happiness.

IN DARK WATERS by Mary Burton

Kelsey Warren had fled her home town years ago to get away from Sheriff Mitch Garrett—a man who claimed he didn't love her. Now Kelsey is back, and eager to solve the mystery surrounding her mother's disappearance. Amidst uncovering clues, the two hit it off once again. This time round, was Mitch in it for the long haul?

On sale from 15th December 2006

Available at WHSmith, Tesco, ASDA, Borders, Eason, Sainsbury's and most bookshops

www.silhouette.co.uk

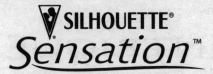

1206/18b

PAWN by Carla Cassidy

Bombshell—Athena Force

Lynn White had been used as a pawn in the past—but now, close to the Athena Academy, and with a life of her own, she was determined that no one would use her again. But as her past returned to haunt her, Lynn had to return to the stealth game—and to the man she had loved and lost…

THIRD SIGHT

by Suzanne McMinn

PAX

The PAX League had saved Riley Tremaine's life and turned him into a special terrorism-fighting superagent with a special gift for sight, but it had cost him the love of his life, Nina Philips. Now Nina was in grave danger and the secret that had torn them apart might just save her life.

BULLETPROOF PRINCESS

by Vicki Hinze

Bombshell—The IT Girls

For modern-day princess Chloe St John, working undercover for the Gotham Rose spies was the perfect chance to prove herself in the face of her mother's constant criticisms. But nothing in Chloe's royal upbringing prepared her to take down a criminal mastermind…and a fellow Rose who might be betraying her to the enemy.

On sale from 15th December 2006

Available at WHSmith, Tesco, ASDA, Borders, Eason,
Sainsbury's and most bookshops

www.silhouette.co.uk

GEN/46/RTL9

INTRIGUE™

Breathtaking romantic suspense

4 brand-new titles each month

Available on the third Friday of every month
from WHSmith, ASDA, Tesco
and all good bookshops
www.silhouette.co.uk

M036/TFK

WHEN SHE OPENED THE DOOR TO A FRIEND, WAS SHE UNKNOWINGLY GIVING REFUGE TO A KILLER?

Living in a former monastery, Abby Northrup runs an underground safe haven for abused women and children. But when an old friend and her daughter appear looking for somewhere to stay, Abby finds herself trapped in a world of murder and conspiracy. On the run, Abby must decide which of her beliefs are worth dying for—and which are not...

On sale 17th November 2006

FREE!
4 Books
and a surprise gift!

We would like to take this opportunity to thank you for reading this Silhouette® book by offering you the chance to take FOUR more specially selected titles from the Sensation™ series absolutely FREE! We're also making this offer to introduce you to the benefits of the Mills & Boon® Reader Service™—

★ **FREE home delivery**
★ **FREE gifts and competitions**
★ **FREE monthly Newsletter**
★ **Exclusive Reader Service offers**
★ **Books available before they're in the shops**

Accepting these FREE books and gift places you under no obligation to buy, you may cancel at any time, even after receiving your free shipment. Simply complete your details below and return the entire page to the address below. You don't even need a stamp!

YES! Please send me 4 free Sensation books and a surprise gift. I understand that unless you hear from me, I will receive 6 superb new titles every month for just £3.10 each, postage and packing free. I am under no obligation to purchase any books and may cancel my subscription at any time. The free books and gift will be mine to keep in any case.

S6ZEF

Ms/Mrs/Miss/Mr .... Initials ....

Surname .... **BLOCK CAPITALS PLEASE**

Address ....

....

.... Postcode ....

Send this whole page to:
UK: FREEPOST CN81, Croydon, CR9 3WZ

Offer valid in UK only and is not available to current Mills & Boon® Reader Service™ subscribers to this series. Overseas and Eire please write for details. We reserve the right to refuse an application and applicants must be aged 18 years or over. Only one application per household. Terms and prices subject to change without notice. Offer expires 28th February 2007. As a result of this application, you may receive offers from Harlequin Mills & Boon and other carefully selected companies. If you would prefer not to share in this opportunity please write to The Data Manager, PO Box 676, Richmond, TW9 1WU.

Silhouette® is a registered trademark owned and used under licence.
Sensation™ is being used as a trademark. The Mills & Boon® Reader Service™ is being used as a trademark.